WANTED

KARPOV KINRADE

LIV CHATHAM

http://KarpovKinrade.com

I'm recording everything that happens in the very likely scenario that my whole plan goes to shit and all that's left to tell the story is this journal. If you're reading this, I'm probably dead, and it's too late to do anything about any of it now. But, at least, you'll know the truth. And I won't hold back. I won't try to make myself look better than I am. I have no delusions about myself.

I began the day stealing from a department store and ended with lying to my new boss.

I'm no saint, but I'm far from the worst that exists. No, there are much worse specimens of humanity than me. They're the ones to be afraid of and the kind I'm trying to get away *from*. But I don't think it's going to work.

After all, nothing in my life has ever worked.

I'm not trying to wallow in self-pity. I'm just being honest. Some lives shine with a kind of preternatural luck that follows them around. Others live under a perpetual storm cloud.

My life is the latter.

But who knows, maybe the weather is turning in my favor for once.

You never know, right?

STEAL A LITTLE AND THEY'LL JAIL YOUR ASS, steal a lot and they'll make you queen. It's a Bob Dylan quote with my personal spin on a few of the words. And it's all I could think about as I walked casually through the exit of the department store with new as-yet-paid-for dress and shoes shoved into my oversized purse.

It was only a borrow. I'll return them tomorrow.

However, stores generally frown on you taking their shit without paying, so I schooled my face into a bored housewife expression and causally browsed a few items lining the back of the store on my way out.

Why do they put shit past the checkout stands? You don't pass them when you come in, only when you go out, and by then you've already paid. What's the point?

Fortunately for me, the store alarm didn't go off. No one tried to stop me. In fact, one of the employees nodded his head in my direction with a smile as I left. "Have a nice day," he said with a wink. "And come back again soon."

He looked college-aged, with a sweet grin and kind brown eyes.

"Thanks," I said blandly, not giving into the temptation to flirt back.

He was cute and it could have been fun, but he looked too innocent to handle the skeletons piling up in my closet. And by the time this blistering summer is over, there will be more.

I sighed deeply once I was safely in my beaten-up old car, doors closed and locked, air conditioning drying the sweat dotting my skin.

I studied my hands gripping the steering wheel as they shook, my fingernails bitten down to stumps, my cuticles in need of some serious TLC. You'd think this was my first time stealing, the way my heart fluttered in my chest like a hummingbird on crack.

Closing my eyes, I steadied myself with a few deep breaths.

A sharp knock on the window startled me back to the present and scared the living hell out of me.

It was the cute store guy.

Jesus.

I rolled down my window and put on my best 'polite but I'm in a hurry' smile. "Is something wrong?"

If I got caught, I'd be ruined, and I wouldn't be the only one to suffer.

He held up a cell phone. "I think you left this in the store?"

With a relieved sigh, I took it from him, feeling twice the idiot. How could I be so stupid? "Thank you. It must've fallen from my purse."

This time, my smile was one hundred percent genuine. Losing my phone would have been Bad-with-a-capital-B.

He glanced inside my car, towards said purse, but fortunately, I'd zipped it shut, the stolen items safely tucked out of sight.

"Hey, so, I was wondering…" he began.

I inwardly cringed, just knowing what was next. Could I start the car and hightail it out there fast enough? *Would* I?

Then, he stunned me with a nervous slur of, "Would you like to grab a coffee after my shift?"

I blinked. "Thanks, but I have a job interview today." This was it? Really?

His smile faltered. "Oh, right. Well, good luck."

Before he could ask for my number, I rolled up my window, waved, and then drove off.

A quick glance in the rearview mirror revealed him standing there, a bit forlorn. He watched my car leave the lot before he turned back toward the store.

"Your lucky day, bud," I muttered under my breath.

Boys like troubled girls before they know what kind of trouble they're really in for. I'd just saved him a shit ton of heartache.

My phone binged just as I pulled up to the curb and parked in front of my house. I already knew who it was, and a blanket of depression dropped over me as I checked the messages, proving myself right.

ARE YOU READY?

WITH SHAKING HANDS, I REPLIED.

YES.

. . .

GOOD.

I SAT THERE, WAITING FOR THE THREE DOTS TO blink, signaling a reply, but when nothing appeared on the tiny screen, I felt the anger beginning to bubble. That was it? That was all I was going to get? I mentally screamed a few choice words at the sender of the texts, then grabbed my purse and headed into the house.

I heard the sound of an argument even before I set foot on the cracked concrete steps. One kick of the screen door later, I was in the living room, tense and ready.

My father, a tall brute of a man with beady eyes, a rounded stomach fed by liquor, and meaty fists, towered over my little brother, wielding a broken beer bottle like a knife.

"You do as you're told," he was shouting. "Or I'll shove this so far up your ass you'll be eating glass and shit for a *week*."

My little brother stood there, trembling, with his thin forearm protecting his face. At fourteen, he was small for his age and much preferred reading books to fighting.

As my father lurched forward to backhand my brother, I shoved Jeremy aside and stepped between them.

The blow jarred my teeth and pain exploded across my cheekbone. If there weren't any broken bones, I'd be shocked. I choked, clutching my face as tears stung my eyes.

My dad's eyes widened. "What are you doing, you little slut?" He snarled, sending spittle straight at me. "You're nothing but a worthless whore." He stumbled to the couch to grab another beer.

Now was my chance, before he could wind himself up for another strike, a strike I sure as hell wasn't going to be around to take. I grabbed Jeremy by the arm and dragged him out of the room to our shared bedroom at the end of the hall before that blow could land.

Once locked in the safety of our shared bedroom, I checked him over quickly. "Are you okay? Did he hurt you?"

Jeremy shook his head, but tears glistened in his large eyes.

My heart broke and I pulled him close, hugging him tight. "I'll get us out of this. I promise." And I would get us out, by any means necessary, even if it involved me dying.

My little brother's shoulders shook in mute sobs, silent as they must be in this house. We are the children of the silent pain. I grimaced. If nothing else, Children of the Silent Pain would be a cool band name.

When he calmed down, I released him and wiped his face with my sleeve. "I have to go, but you should climb out the window and stay at Rick's tonight. Go to school with him in the morning."

Jeremy's caramel eyes widened. "But won't you get in trouble if I leave?"

"I'll be fine. Don't worry about me. I can take care of myself," I said. We are twelve years apart, and I only came back to this hell hole to rescue him. Well… mostly for him. I had a plan. Kind of. I shoved him toward the window. "Now, go!"

He nodded and detoured to grab his backpack, then returned to the window and climbed out.

I exhaled and turned my attention back to my father. He had the TV in the living room on as loud as it could go and now, he was bellowing at the game.

Hoping he'd remain distracted, I crept down the hall and snuck into the kitchen with as much stealth as I could muster. After snagging a bag of frozen peas from the freezer and grabbing the ibuprofen, I scuttled back to my bedroom and locked the door.

Suddenly drained, I collapsed on my bed and then slid to the floor, pressing the frozen peas to my cheek.

I tried to cry.

I wanted to cry.

Hell, I *needed* to cry.

But... nothing. I felt dead inside—and that scared me more than anything.

I needed to feel. *Do* something to numb the pain that shriveled my soul, made me feel like I was a shell of a person, already dead, a ghost of myself haunting my own life.

I felt under my bed until my fingers tripped over the small silver box that held a razor blade and alcohol wipes. Still numb, I pulled it out and flipped open the lid. It took only a second to clean the blade, and then, I was pulling my shorts up as far as I could, eyeing the small white scars crisscrossing my inner thighs.

With a deep breath, I pressed the metal blade into my flesh, gently at first, then with more pressure until I felt the skin brake under that sharp edge of pain.

Crimson blood spilled and dripped down my pale leg.

Relief surged through me, almost as if the seeping blood released the poison lurking in my soul. I sighed as the tears finally began to fall.

I'm not proud of it, and I'm not writing for sympathy. But I promised I wouldn't paint myself in a false, flattering light, and I'm keeping my word—at least, in this instance.

Carefully, I cleaned myself with an alcohol wipe, applied a bandage, and then shoved the container back under my bed.

It was time to move on. I had an interview. I opened my purse and grabbed my 'borrowed' outfit, a conservative navy-blue, button-up dress with matching slip-on ballet shoes. Everything fit to a T and minutes later, I stood in front of the mirror, staring at the image reflected there.

"Not bad," I murmured. No, I looked damn good. Striking, even. The color brought out the blue in my eyes and complemented my dark hair and fair skin. Of course, I could still see the tattoos on my arms, but as practically everyone had them these days, I didn't see how that would be a problem.

Then, I glanced at my cheek and winced outright at the dramatic array of reds and blues standing out against my white skin in a nice bruise despite the ice and meds.

It took a good twenty minutes to do my makeup, thanks to the purple spreading over my cheekbone. I flinched each time I dabbed on the concealer, but finally, I'd finished and even I couldn't tell I'd been hit. I just had to keep my fingers crossed that my eye wouldn't swell. Then, there'd be no hiding my injury.

After one last dab of lip gloss, I followed my brother's path and shimmied through the window. I made it back to my car and then I was off again, before my father knew I'd even left.

It was dusk by the time I reached the address for my interview. I switched off the engine and settled in my car, preparing to wait, as instructed, until full darkness descended.

I didn't mind. It gave me the chance to study the mansion I'd be cleaning, provided I got the job, of course.

The place was massive, by far the largest and remotest estate in and around our small town. A forest of trees blanketed the mansion from the road and you had to drive down a long, winding driveway before you'd even catch a glimpse of the slate tile roof. It wasn't until the last bend, when you were upon the place that you got a good view.

Other than the ornately carved tall, black double arched front door, the mansion was entirely white with stately columns that gave it a Roman villa vibe. Fountains graced the lawn and a meticulous garden of red roses lined the walkway from the drive to the front door.

For a place that had been vacant forever, it looked remarkably well kept. The man who'd bought it last month was a mystery in our small Northern California town. No one had seen him, but everyone had heard the rumors of his wealth and that he'd paid for the place in cash. With that kind of money, he had to be dripping with diamonds. He'd have to be to buy the place. Few could afford it, and those who could didn't want it after... well, after everything went down. A real estate agent is required by law to disclose when a murder's been committed on a property. That typically doesn't help sell a place.

I sat in my car, tapping a beat on the steering wheel as I watched and waited. Finally, the sun sank out of view and when the full moon hung over the treetops, fully visible, I checked my phone and scanned the job details one last time.

Job details. Check. Like I hadn't had them memorized already. Well, there was nothing left to do but get the show on the road.

Inhaling a deep breath, I exited my car and walked to the entrance. After lifting the brass knocker and giving the door a sharp rap, I rubbed my sweating palms against my thigh without thinking. Damnit. I'd just left a dark wet smudge on the borrowed dress.

I drew a deep breath and glanced around. I'd been here, at the house, once before, but it wasn't a night I liked to recall.

Fortunately, the door opened, sparing me the memories, and I straightened my spine and tried to act like someone else. Someone poised, polished, and well-spoken. Someone who deserved to scrub the toilets of the filthy rich.

A tall, rail thin man wearing a traditional butler uniform greeted me. "You must be Miss Kassandra Blackwood," he said as he ushered me inside. "Welcome."

"Thanks... er...thank you," I replied, belatedly polishing my speech so I could later polish the silver here.

My phone buzzed in my purse, and I scowled at the annoyance.

The butler's eyes flicked down, but he said nothing. Instead, he escorted me to a small room a few doors to the left of the foyer and offered me a seat on a plush leather chair. "Please, wait a moment. The Count will be right with you."

Count? I raised an eyebrow. Had he said… Count? Just who the hell *was* this guy? I scanned the room assessing the value of the rugs, furniture, and knickknacks in a cursory calculation. It didn't take long to determine that, most likely, just one of the knickknacks on his shelf was worth more than my whole life. I couldn't imagine being so wealthy that you'd spend insane amounts of money on painted eggs or some shit just to display them behind locked glass doors. It was vulgar.

But who was I to judge? After all, I didn't have two pennies to rub together.

Then, the butler returned, and I stood as he smiled and gestured for me to follow. "Right this way."

He led me through gilded hallways with more molding than wall, and past rooms filled to the brim with priceless antiques. Obviously, the Count had changed a lot about the house since I'd been there last.

Finally, the butler escorted me into an office lined wall-to-wall with leather-bound books. The room was dark and very Gothic, without windows. The only sources of light were the ornate iron candelabras, each boasting five beeswax pillar candles. Strange. The room was an odd choice considering the rest of the mansion had electricity.

Under any other circumstances, I'd have hightailed it out of there. The whole place screamed sexual-assault-that-gets-thrown-out-of-court—that is, if it ever made to court in the first place with me. After all, they'd take one look at how I'm dressed and then another at my past and conclude I'd clearly asked for it.

Yet the more I inspected the place, the more the highly tuned street-smart side of me kept telling the rest of me to calm down, that it wasn't getting any real rapey vibes.

I hesitated, on the fence, but deep inside, I knew I couldn't just walk away. I didn't have a choice.

Trusting the street-smarts knew what they were talking about, I stepped inside.

Immediately, the butler left, closing the door behind him with a click.

It was then I saw the man, standing in the shadows. As I watched, he emerged into the circle of candlelight, book in hand.

It took a moment for my eyes to adjust to the lighting, but when they did, my jaw dropped.

He was tall, at least 6'3", and elegantly lean in a black suit tailored to his trim, muscular frame. Yet it was his face that drew my gaze, so fine, ageless, and all chiseled angles. His dark, nearly black eyes glinted in the candlelight or perhaps with a hint of madness.

He looked so elegant, suave, and fierce at once.

He snapped his book shut and set it on a nearby shelf, his gaze never once leaving mine. "Good evening, Miss Blackwood," he said as he reached out his hand in greeting.

A shiver ran up my spine the instant our hands met, and almost at once, a wave of unexpected desire rolled over me, making my legs tremble and taking me by surprise. Shocked, I drew a silent, fortifying breath and stood firm, willing myself not to flinch under his gaze or touch. "Thank you for the interview, Mr. ...?" I never got a name. Just an address.

He tilted his head, causing a lock of dark hair to fall across his forehead as his long, elegant fingers tightened ever so slightly around my hand. "It's Count... actually."

I narrowed my eyes. "That's rather grandiose," I teased and then promptly bit my lip. *Don't freaking forget your place, Kass.*

Fortunately, he didn't appear offended, judging by the wry smile that curved his lips, anyway. "It is a title well-earned," he said mildly. Then, his eyes dropped to my hand, still clutched in his, and I stared

16

at the line of his thick, black lashes as he studied the ink on my arm.

Suddenly self-conscious, I pulled free of his grasp. Instantly, part of me felt a loss at the lack of contact, which was, of course, a shit-ton of pure stupidness, so I mentally clocked myself in the head, hoping to knock some sense into my brain.

"Please, sit," the Count waved a hand at a tufted leather chair as he took the seat behind the mahogany desk nearby. "Tell me, Kassandra. May I call you Kassandra?"

To be perfectly honest, the way he said my name made me a bit lightheaded. I sat down, mentally kicking myself again and forced my mind back to the interview. For the first time, I realized he'd never actually told me his name, but now it felt weird to ask again. "My friends call me Kass," I said, clearing my throat. "But Kassandra is fine too."

"Tell me, Kassandra, why are you applying for this job?"

This was it, my moment to shine. I looked him straight in the eye and recited from memory the script I'd been given to say, "I'm passionate about house-keeping and finding new and innovative ways to keep a home clean and inviting. I'm organized, strong, and can work long hours without tiring." Ha! What a crock. "I would be an asset to any house." There, I'd nailed every word *and* emotion.

The Count leaned back, steepled his fingers, and studied me in the candlelight. The flickering of flames lent him a menacing look but strangely, that only somehow amplified the attraction I felt. This wasn't an innocent boy who didn't know which way was up. This was a man… a man who had clearly walked with darkness and lived to tell the tale—and a man who obviously knew his way around a woman, maybe even women with my kind of demons. My libido warmed at that, a libido that had been very much neglected of late due to my inability to make good decisions on the men front. Yet, while I was a year into taking a sabbatical from men entirely, my libido whispered I just might want to make an exception for *this* tall drink of water.

Then, I became suddenly aware of the silence hanging heavy in the room and the fact that the Count was just sitting there, watching me.

I gritted my teeth. *Quit thinking with your pants and think with your head, Kass.*

As if aware I was suddenly paying attention again, the Count arched a cool brow and said in a low, menacing voice, "I have three rules for anyone who works with me or lives with me, Kassandra."

I froze as a prickle of foreboding crept down my neck.

"The first rule, Kassandra, is no lying. Ever. Without exception. So, before I terminate this interview and have you escorted out, I will give you one more chance to answer my question. Why are you applying for this job? This time, I want the truth."

He never raised his voice, but there was such power behind his words I felt compelled to obey, and that terrified the ever-loving shit out of me.

This was the moment I should have gotten the hell out of there. But I didn't. I couldn't.

Still, I needed to know what I was playing with, so I asked, "And what are the other two rules?"

His dark brows creased with displeasure. "We will go over those should you get the job."

It was my turn to frown. What a freaking strange interview. I sucked in a breath as I prepared a suitable combination of the truth. Then, I smiled, knowing exactly what I'd say. After all, a lie is always most believable when it contains a kernel of truth, and my lie had the advantage of being entirely true and entirely a lie at the exact same time.

"The truth is, I came back home after being gone for some time to help take care of my little brother after my mother died. I need a job, and this town isn't exactly overflowing with them. I'm a shit house-keeper and I couldn't care less about 'innovative cleaning techniques', but I *am* a hard worker and I will learn to do what you want and do it well, should you hire me." Let's see what he did with that. I raised an eyebrow at him as if to say, "*ball's in your court, buddy.*"

He studied me for a long time. I didn't know if he was waiting for me to crack or what, but I didn't play his game. I just sat patiently, waiting. I could do that all night.

Finally, he smiled. It was brief, and it didn't reach his eyes entirely. Eyes that looked weighed down with so much pain it couldn't be hidden.

"Very well, Miss Blackwood, you're hired. You may move in tonight and start tomorrow."

"Thank you, I—" I paused as his words sank in. "Wait, what? Move in?"

He nodded. "Were you not aware? This is a live-in position. That's non-negotiable. Will that be a problem?"

I gulped. *Yes.* "No, not at all."

I plastered a smile on my face but inwardly I was already swearing at myself. *What the hell are you going to do now? You're really up shit creek, Kass.*

2

The third time my phone buzzed, Leonard's eyes dropped to my purse. "Feel free to attend to your personal business, Miss Kassandra. You will not offend."

I gave the butler a half smile of soft thanks and pulled out the phone. I'd much rather ignore it, ignore *him,* but I knew I'd have to deal with him at some point. Might as well get it over with.

He'd sent several texts and I scanned them all quickly.

Update. Now.

NOW.

I'm not a patient man, Kassy. You should know that.

WHAT THE HELL IS GOING ON, KASS?

My reply was brief and to the point.

I got the job. Back off. Everything's going as planned. I'll get you what you need. You just better deliver on your part of the deal.

His response was immediate.

Check in daily. Or else. You know what happens to traitors.

I shoved the phone back into my purse, trying my best to ignore his threat but my body wouldn't let me. My pulse quickened and even though the mansion was cool, sweat beaded my forehead. Flashbacks of the last time I was in this house hit me with brutal force.

A high school party with no parents.

Alcohol and drugs.

I drank too much and felt sick. Too sick.

He offered to help me to a bedroom to rest.

Then he didn't leave.

I reported the rape, and the next day I was pulled into a car, taken to the woods and beaten so badly I missed school for two weeks recovering.

I was blindfolded and couldn't identify the guilty.

But I knew.

I also learned my lessons that night.

1: Guys who offer to help always want something.

2: Snitches get stitches.

"Is everything okay, Miss Kassandra?" Leonard's quiet voice yanked me from the past.

I blinked and shoved those memories back into the depths of my mind as far as I could. "Yes, everything is perfect." I said with all the charm I could muster. "But you don't need to drive me. I can drive myself. It'll be easier that way."

Leonard frowned. "I wouldn't hear of it. I shall drive you and be of assistance in any way I can, as instructed by the Count."

The tone of his voice and the way he worried his lip made me realize that he was desperate to do his job well, so I reluctantly conceded. But Jesus, this was not going to be a good scene if my dad was home and drunk.

And before I wasted another minute, I needed to warn Jeremy I wouldn't be living there anymore.

"Just give me one sec," I said.

Leonard nodded and turned to afford me some privacy as once again, I texted madly into my phone.

Stay a few days with your friend. I got a job, but it's live-in. I'll keep you safe, I promise. Love you.

Jeremy responded at once, and his response broke my heart.

I can only stay maybe two nights before the parents get suspicious. What should I do after that?

Go to another friend's house?

I can't. No one else.

Shit.

I'll figure something out. Just don't go home while dad's there.

We made quick time to my house, and Leonard didn't raise an eyebrow at my neighborhood or my passed-out, drunk asshole of a father on the couch.

The butler followed me to my bedroom and stood at the door, almost as if on guard, as I threw everything I owned—which admittedly wasn't much—into a bag that I tossed over my shoulder. "Ready," I said.

"Is that all you wish to take?" he asked politely.

"It's all I own," I said. "So… yeah."

He nodded and with a gentlemanly nod of his head, took the bag from me and carried it down the hall.

We'd almost made a clean escape when the snoring from the couch turned to a series of coughs and my dad awoke. His eyes narrowed into slits as he sat up. "What the hell do you think you're doing, you little bitch?"

I paled as shame and rage leapt to life inside me. At my side, Leonard went ramrod straight and for a slight man who didn't look inclined to fighting a dude twice his size, he didn't seem the least bit worried or scared.

Curious. And impressive. Leonard instantly rose in my esteem.

"I'm leaving," I told my father.

My dad glanced between me and Leonard, clearly trying to assess the threat.

Leonard nodded politely. "Shall we go, Miss Blackwood?"

"You're not taking my daughter anywhere," my dad slurred.

I snorted at that. "He's not taking me, I'm leaving. And you can't stop me. I'm an adult." Reason never worked with him, and since I didn't want this to lead to an altercation, I followed up with a threat. "If you try to stop me, the cops will be here before you know it."

My dad hesitated, and I knew that was my chance.

I hurried to the door, but Leonard was there first, holding it open. I dashed through and he was close behind. We made it to the car and down the street before my dad left the house. By then, it was too late.

I exhaled deeply as we zoomed down the road.

"I'm sorry about that," I said. The words slipped off my tongue by rote programming. I've spent my entire life apologizing for my father and my family. Apologizing for daring to exist.

"You are not responsible for the actions of others," the butler replied.

His words surprised me, and I gave him a smile then leaned back in the leather seat and closed my eyes. My cheekbone still hurt from the run-in earlier, and I could feel the swelling getting worse. Tomorrow, the puffiness and probably even the bruise would be hard to hide. Still, I didn't regret it. Not for a second. What would such a blow have done to Jeremy? I shuddered, knowing I'd take any number of beatings for him.

Unwilling to spare another thought on my dad, I forced my thoughts in a different direction and glanced at the butler. "Can I ask you something?"

"You may. I will answer if I can."

"What's the Count like to work for?" And live with. My bedroom had better have a lock on the door —and windows.

There was a long pause. "The Count is a very private person. As long as you follow his rules, you'll be fine."

"And what are those rules?" I asked. "Besides no lying."

"He wishes to tell you himself when we return."

Leonard wasn't exaggerating. The moment we returned the butler ushered me directly into the Count's office even before taking my bag to my room.

Again, the Count stood in the candlelight, an enigma of fierceness and beauty. "You will clean in the evenings and have the days for rest, is that understood?"

Weird but whatever. I nodded.

"And you will follow the rules I set," he continued.

"And those would be?"

He placed a scroll—an honest to god scroll—in front of me. It was embossed in gold filigree, and written in calligraphy, were three rules:

I swear never to lie.

I swear never to steal.

I swear never to disobey.

There was an X and a line, presumably for my signature.

"Do you agree to these rules?" he asked.

"Never disobey?" I repeated the last line, a flutter of nerves churning my stomach. Obedience has never been my strong suit.

"That is the requirement for working here," he said in a voice that brooked no discussion.

I pushed the paper away and shook my head.

"Unquestioning obedience is unreasonable," I objected. "I'm an employee not a slave."

"So, you're turning down the job?" Was that an incredulous note in his voice?

This all smelled of something dangerous. Damnit, I should have run the instant I saw his candlelit room.

My phone chose that moment to buzz again and the Count's eyes fell on my purse. "You will also relinquish your cell phone while you are on my property," he said. "And any other recording or communication devices."

What the hell? "Why?"

"I value my privacy," he replied without elaboration.

I pulled my purse onto my shoulder. "I don't think this is going to work out, after all," I said. I was only half bluffing. The consequences of walking out on this were too high. I knew this. I had to take the job, no matter what he demanded of me, but *shit*, this was seriously messed up.

"Very well, you're free to go," he said with a dismissive wave of his hand.

Was he bluffing? Who the hell knew? It wasn't like he needed me. Surely, there were a shit-ton more qualified candidates than me, anyway.

But then again… all the strange rules.

I stood, deciding he was bluffing after all. "It was a pleasure meeting you, Count. And good luck on your hunt for a housekeeper. It's hard to find good help in this town. Most people work on weed farms or don't want to work at all."

I turned to leave, measuring my steps to the door, counting every second until he gave in.

The door loomed closer. And closer. I was an inch away from the doorknob.

Hell, that's what I got for playing chicken with an enigma.

I was going to lose.

The Count cleared his throat. "Would you like to know what your salary would have been? Before you leave?"

Bastard.

I stopped and turned, raising an eyebrow. "Sure. How much do you pay your slaves?"

He stood and walked to a large painting on the wall, an oil from the looks of it that depicted a dragon protecting a beautiful woman wearing a sword. He slid the painting aside to reveal a safe, and with fast fingers, deftly plugged in the security code.

The door swung open on well-oiled hinges and I tensed, craning to see the contents without looking too obvious. I caught a good glimpse of piles of cash before he closed the safe and returned to his desk with a small black chest accented with rubies and emeralds. Were they real? That would be extra! Slowly, he opened the lid, revealing the box stuffed with cash, all one-hundred dollar bills.

"You must be a favorite with the IRS, paying in cash like that," I said, but I took a reluctant step forward. That was more money than I'd ever had in my life.

He took a small stack of cash from the box and set it on the table. "Each month you will receive $7,000, cash, for your work," he said, placing another smaller stack next to the first. "And if you do your job exceptionally well, you will also receive a $3,000 bonus."

Ten thousand dollars a month to clean his house? That was a fortune.

"What's the catch? Why are you paying so much for a housekeeper?" Then, I folded my arms and looked him directly in the eye. "Are you expecting sex?" I asked bluntly. "In my experience, men always want something for their money."

I'd like to say that if he had wanted sex, I'd be out. That I had a line. But when it came to this, I couldn't afford to have a line. Not if I wanted to save my brother.

The Count's dark eyes searched my face. "Firstly, I am not like any man you've ever met, Miss Black-wood, I can assure you of that. And secondly, I do, in fact, want something for my money. I want a clean house, and someone who can serve and prepare drinks when I have guests. The rest of the money is for your discretion. What happens here stays here."

"Illegal shit?" I raised a suspicious brow. "I can't be involved in illegal shit."

"Your record would beg to differ," he countered softly, "but no, nothing illegal. Just private."

"You looked into my record?" I asked, feeling both embarrassed and angry. Both were a combination of emotions I'd become well-acquainted with over the course of my life.

His face was an unreadable mask. "Of course I did. How would I consider you for a live-in position if I hadn't done my due diligence?"

I cocked my hip, studying the devilishly hand-some man before me. "Then you know I'm not squeaky clean. Why risk it?"

He stood and walked around his desk to sit on the edge and face me. We were so close that our knees brushed and my pulse leapt at the contact.

Focus, Kass. Focus, damnit.

"I am not the one taking the risks here. I know

what I'm getting," the Count informed me coolly. "Do you?"

I frowned and forced my mind back on track. Yes, this could be a good gig for me, providing it was legit. With this kind of cash, I could take care of Jeremy long-term.

But in my experience, if it was too good to be true, you're probably going to get screwed.

But the money... I could put up with a lot if it meant giving my brother a better life.

And I was going to blow it all, as usual, by walking away.

God damnit.

Still.

Shit.

A smile teased the corner of his mouth. "Should I assume you're reconsidering the offer?"

I licked my lips, my gaze riveted to the stacks of money. "So, I could earn up to $10,000 a month? Just for cleaning this place?"

"Yes. And fulfilling other responsibilities, as needed, all within reasonable standards," he said. "But you must agree to follow the rules. At the first hint of breaking them, you're out. No excuses, no exceptions."

"I agree," I said, trying not to choke on the lie as I took my seat before him once again.

"Then sign." He handed me a pen.

It was a fountain pen and it looked ancient. When I pressed the sharpened tip on the paper to write, nothing came out. Frustrated, I shook it and said, "It's not working."

"You must sign in your own blood," he clarified, like this was a totally normal and obvious thing to do when agreeing on employment. Then, he took the pen from me and pricked my finger with the tip before I could move.

"Ouch!" I gasped, pulling my hand away from his. "What the hell?"

Unruffled, he merely handed the pen back. "Now, sign."

I hesitated. Was I insane? Yeah, probably. Did I have a choice in all this? No, not really. Knowing I was going to regret it, I took the pen and once again pushed down on the paper. This time, it worked, and when I signed, it was in red blood that darkened as it dried.

A wave of nausea rolled over me and I swallowed back the bile rising in my throat. I couldn't vomit here. Not now. Not under the probing gaze of the ridiculously sexy man before me.

"Welcome to your new home," the Count said as my stomach churned. "Leonard will get you settled in your quarters tonight and give you a tour, then tomorrow evening you will begin work."

I nodded, rose to my feet and turned back toward the door.

"Your phone?"

Damnit. I'd hoped he'd forget. I sighed. "I need to text someone first. I can't just disappear without contact," I said, turning around. I was standing firm on this point, whatever he said. I wouldn't put Jeremy through that. We'd find another way.

But if there were another way, I'd already have found it.

Shit.

I waited for him to respond.

"Very well." He nodded. "Send your final texts, then hand it over. You may retrieve your device when you leave, but you may not use it within the confines of my property, is that understood?"

A feeling welled up inside me, a feeling I resented, one I'd grown up with. It's the same feeling you get being sent to the principal's office for a proper scolding.

And defending yourself always made it worse.

I would know.

I bit my tongue, tasting blood, and then nodded, holding all my resentment inside. Even still, it was hard to ignore the mesmerizing pull he had on me even while I was caught playing his game. Because make no mistake, this was all a game. The stakes were just higher for me than for him, which he undoubtedly knew as a filthy rich person, the kind that likes to use their money as whips to control the poor.

Turning my back on him, I texted Jeremy first.

I can't explain, but I won't have my phone on me a lot of the time. I'm sorry. But I'll check my messages whenever I can, so reach out if you need me. Stay safe. Stay away from dad. Do what you have to do to survive, kiddo. I'm going to take care of you. I promise.

The next text was much harder to send.

I'm in. Can't keep my phone on me… boss's rules or I would have lost the job. Don't expect regular check-ins. Not my fault. Honor our deal or I'm out.

I turned off the phone, knowing they were both likely responding that instant, and knowing it would be some time before I could answer. God, this would kill me.

"Fine, here," I said, holding out my phone to the Count.

Our fingers brushed as he took it from my hand and damnit, the shivers returned, tracing up my spine in a flush of desire. I jerked back, vowing to avoid him as much as I could. "You said I'd get some money up front," I reminded him. If he was going to be a stickler for the rules, then so would I.

He nodded, once, and removed a stack of cash from the treasure box and handed it to me. "As promised."

I took it from him and ran a finger over the bills, counting them.

It was so much money. More than I'd ever held at once.

But it wasn't enough. Not by a long shot. Not to get me out of the mess I was in.

I tucked it in my purse and walked to the door, feeling the Count's eyes on my back with each step I took. It was difficult to resist the impulse to look back one last time. But I couldn't let him have that much sway over me.

So I stayed strong and kept my eyes forward. But, oh my heavens, it was hard.

Once in the hall, I darted into the nearest room, closed the door quickly behind me and slumped against it, releasing a gasp of breath I'd held in for too long. My head spun from the entire encounter, but more importantly, *just what had I done?*

I had a knack for getting myself into shit-filled

messes, but this particular mess was brewing to be the worst of them all.

Still, I patted my purse. There was a lot of money in this mansion—especially in that safe of his. And from what I'd seen, that stash could solve nearly all my problems.

After taking a few deep, calming breaths, I emerged back into the hall and returned to the foyer where Leonard waited.

"Would you care for a tour, Miss Kassandra?" he asked.

"Please."

He spun smartly on his heel and proceeded to give me a brief tour of the place. I drank in every detail like a man lost in the desert who finally discovered water. There was so much...and much of it strange. A crystal fountain that produced a soft white smoke rather than water. Art pieces and sculptures that looked ancient, but instead of the normal religious figures from those times, these all sported creatures of fantasy. The doors were unusually tall, and there were so many rooms. Had the Count actually built on to the place? The kitchen was huge, fit for a host of gourmet chefs to compete at once. There was so much I lost count of it all, several dining rooms, a formal living room, and even a media room with a wall-sized television that rivaled most movie theaters. Then, the ballroom, a gym, a short walk through the gardens outside complete with Zen mazes, and back to a library stacked with books... There was even a forge with an anvil.

"Who uses the forge?" I asked unable to believe my eyes.

"The Count. He enjoys his hobbies from time to time," Leonard said.

The appraiser in me put a value on every knick-knack, every painting, every hand-woven rug, tapestry, sculpture *and* artifact I'd seen. The numbers were staggering. It was beyond tempting, but I couldn't touch any of it. I had to keep my hands clean for my Jeremy plan to work. At least, for now. Until... And then? At any rate, desperate times called for desperate measures, and all that.

The Count would survive what I was about to do to him.

And it wasn't like I had a choice. Me and my brother would lose everything if I didn't follow through.

People like to imagine that there *are* always choices in life. That one can always choose the moral course. That one *should* always choose the moral superior.

But here's what I'd tell those people... until you've walked a mile in my shoes, you don't get to judge.

Because at the end of the day, there's no argument, moral or otherwise, that would convince me a bunch of rich people shit and piles of money are worth more than my brother's life.

And that's what's at stake here.

So those people can shove their moral high horse up their ass.

I'm going to save my brother, even if I have to betray the Count and lose everything else in the process.

The Count gave me three rules.

And I'm about to break them all.

3

I fell in love with my bedroom the moment I stepped through the door. And then I felt guilty, thinking of my brother and what he'd have to do to survive while I was here living like a queen.

The room was huge with a sitting area by a grand fireplace, a balcony with a hammock, a four-poster, canopied bed entwined with ivy, and an old-fashioned antique wardrobe inexplicably stocked with beautiful clothing all my size. Designer shit. All of it. I made a mental note to ask Leonard about the clothes.

But first things first, I took off my 'borrowed' dress and folded it carefully, prepping it for its return to the store. Then, I threw on a ripped Black-Eyed

Peas band t-shirt and sweatpants before tossing myself onto the most comfortable bed I'd ever experienced. It felt like floating on a cloud.

Already, I could tell I'd regret leaving this place, once that time came.

After a half hour, I climbed out of the feathery goodness and stretched. Work didn't start until tomorrow, so I had the night to myself.

But what to do? I didn't feel like going out. Yeah, I should start creating a plan for my mission, but not now. Not yet. Maybe I could have just one night to myself? To not think of all the shit I'm sinking in? To pretend like my life might work out okay?

I sighed and decided it was best to use my newfound time to adjust to my new schedule. I've always been a night owl, so it wouldn't be too hard. And to be honest, I don't sleep well, day or night.

I padded over to the well-stocked bookshelf and pulled a book down. And in minutes, I was curled up under a soft, cozy blanket, reading in front of the fire like it could actually be my life. It made me feel warm and good inside, even if I was only pretending for an evening.

I don't know how much later it was when my grumbling stomach interrupted my story to remind me it had been awhile since I'd actually eaten. I set the book aside and rose, giving the base of my spine a good rub before heading out to find the kitchen.

I found the kitchen, after a few detours—there were so many freaking doors—and once there, it took me a bit to discover where everything was. The place was gourmet, through and through, and everything looked brand new as if it had never been used. Was it all a front? Did they even have any food in here? Geez, was that why Leonard was so thin?

Finally, I did find the fridge—the kind that's hidden inside the wall of cabinetry camouflaged to look just like another cupboard—and while not brimming with food, there was enough real fruit, vegetables, and lunchmeat to at least make a decent sandwich.

The cupboard next to the fridge proved to be a mini bar filled with hard liquor. A bottle of whisky with a white bow and a card with the word 'welcome' stood apart from the rest.

My hand shook as I reached for the whiskey and ran a fingertip over the golden label. Then, I caught myself and pulled back, as if bitten.

It was so hard, so difficult to ignore the powerful, seductive lure of alcohol. I closed my eyes, reliving the burn in my throat, taking away my pain and making me forget, for just a little while, the awfulness of my life...

No. I would *not* give in. Not today. Not right now.

Instead, I yanked open the door of the fridge, grabbed the bread, some meat, cheese, lettuce, tomato, and mayo and put together a turkey sandwich. Sandwich in hand, I continued my exploration of the cupboards.

I was halfway through my meal and nearly done with the cupboard contents when a voice startled me from behind.

"If you make a list of your food preferences, Leonard will ensure they are stocked," the Count's deep baritone rumbled from the doorway. He leaned against the frame, arms loosely crossed over his broad chest, his dark eyes orbs of mystery against his pale, smooth skin.

"Thank you," I said, surprised he wasn't making me—the housekeeper—do the grocery shopping. "Um. I don't drink." I waved in the direction of the whisky with the bow. "Just... If that was meant for me, I don't need it."

The Count went to the refrigerator and pulled out

a bottle of red wine. Silent, he poured himself a glass, and it was the most viscous wine I'd ever seen.

Then, he leaned against the granite island to study me as he sipped from his glass, crimson staining his lips and giving him a macabre look.

I finished my sandwich under his steady gaze, and it was totally not awkward at all. Ha!

"You don't drink? And why is that?" he asked when I was done.

I shot him a look. "That," I said, "is actually none of your business."

He raised an eyebrow at that. But I didn't lie to him, so he really couldn't complain I'd broken one of his precious rules. Not yet, anyways.

He fell silent then, but he still watched my every move.

Finally, I asked, "Why did you hire me?"

"Why wouldn't I?" His dark eyes glittered.

"Because I have no experience, no references, and no... polish," I said, for lack of a better word.

He quietly regarded me for several long moments. "You have an interesting assessment of yourself. Curious." He took another sip of wine. "As to why I hired you... I suppose it is in part because you remind me of someone."

I drew back. "This isn't going to be one of those creepy situations where I look like your mother and so you want to kill me and bury me in your garden, is it?"

Amusement flashed over his face. "I assure you. You do not look like my mother."

I narrowed my eyes. "I was actually more concerned with the part where I end up in pieces, fertilizing your roses."

"It is highly unlikely you will meet your end as a result of working for me," he answered calmly.

"Said that way, it's less reassuring than you might think."

"Anyone expecting reassurance from the likes of me will spend their lives disappointed," he said as he drained his glass of the last drop, rinsed it out, and then put it away. "Good night, Miss Kassandra. You might run into... guests I have from time to time. Please don't be concerned. They shouldn't be a bother to you."

And with that, he left the kitchen.

I exhaled a breath I didn't realize I was holding and then following his example, washed my plate, returned it to the cupboard, and headed back to my bedroom.

Guests? I could only assume he meant women. That shouldn't bother me. After all, I'm just the hired help. But oddly, it did. I couldn't deny the flare of jealousy or the arousal at the thought of just what he might be doing with all these guests.

I shook my head, attempting to clear it of the Count, and threw myself onto my bed.

Only, no matter how I tried, I couldn't stop thinking of him.

Even in my dreams—when I finally managed to fall asleep for a few hours—he haunted me. His dark eyes followed me everywhere, and his mesmerizing charisma drew me deeper into his web of games.

After a restless sleep and despite my best intentions to switch my schedule, I rose with the sun, dressed quickly, then headed downstairs for a much-needed cup of coffee.

To my surprise, all the alcohol in the kitchen from the night before had been removed.

Huh?

Why was that consideration so ridiculously touching? Catching my thoughts straying back to the captivating Count, I reminded myself that I have no room in my life for sentiment. Or kindness.

Not if I want to survive.

I drank my coffee in an unnaturally quiet kitchen and considered my plans for the day. First things first, I had to check on Jeremy. Then, I needed to return what I'd stolen from the store, all before my shift started in the evening. Doable, even with the drive back to town.

As I left the front door, purse in hand, I suddenly realized I was leaving without my phone or even an inkling of an idea of how to get it back. A quick check of the Count's office door revealed it locked, so retrieving my phone myself was clearly a no go. It also meant figuring out the combination to the safe wasn't the only one step in my plan. I'd need the key to the door as well.

In the end, I had to leave without my phone, and I headed to Jeremy's school first to ask that they pull him from class so I could, at least, speak to him.

The woman in the front office wasn't too happy with my request, but she did it, anyways. And a few minutes later, Jeremy appeared, his young, handsome face a mask as he stepped through the door. It was habit, of course. The Blackwood kids don't have the best of luck in school offices.

The instant he saw me, his eyes lit. "Are we leaving?" he asked in a hushed whisper.

"Not yet, but I'm working on it," I promised. I pulled out some cash and discreetly slid it into his hands. "Get a room to stay in if you can't stay with friends. I need more time. Protect yourself."

He shoved the money into his jean pockets. "I got your message. Why don't you have your phone anymore?"

"It's a long story," I said, "and you need to get back to class. Can't let your GPA drop now. Not when we're so close." I ruffled his hair and kissed his forehead. Any other teen boy would have cringed and rolled their eyes, but not Jeremy. I'm all he's got, and vice versa. I'd die for him. Hopefully, he knows that. Hopefully, it'll be enough.

I waited until he headed back to class and then left, ignoring the suspicious glare of the office secretary. At least he'd be safe now, I mentally repeated as I slid back into my car and drove to the department store.

Once I'd returned my dress and shoes by depositing them in the dressing room, I just sat in my car, letting it idle as I calmed my nerves and prepared myself for the next stop.

I wasn't looking forward to my next destination. More like I was dreading it, actually.

It only took a few minutes to reach his house, and

by the time I knocked on the front door, I was shaking from head to toe.

He opened the door, his dark eyes narrowing the instant he saw me. He banged the screen back with a vicious kick, grabbed me roughly by the arm, and pulled me into the house.

I shoved him away as hard as I could and rubbed the soon-to-be bruises where his fingers had been. Like I needed more. "Back the hell off. I can't show up to work covered in marks," I snapped.

"Do you have what I need?" he asked.

I forced myself not to slink back as I pulled what was left from my advance out of my purse. "This is all I could get for now, but if you give me a bit longer, I can get you more. It's just taking time."

He leaned over me, one arm above my head, hand pressed against the wall, pinning me against him as with his other hand, he grabbed my jaw and squeezed tight. "I don't want your pocket change. I want the big payout we talked about. The reason I sent you to this job in the first place. If you don't come through, I'll start taking my interest in blood and body parts, and they won't be yours."

My heart clenched in fear. "There's a safe," I squeaked as he loosened his grip enough for me to talk. "Gemstones and cash. You'll make a fortune."

"Good. Tell me more."

"You need a key to the office and a code for the safe. I don't know about other security measures yet."

"Find out. You have a month."

His hips pressed against mine and I could feel his arousal at having this power over me. I squeezed my eyes shut. I had to get out of here. I couldn't go through this again.

Finally, he let my face go and I pushed him away. "I have to get back to work if you want this pulled off that fast."

I'd taken no more than three steps when he asked, "How's Jeremy doing by the way?" He gave me a sadistic smile. "He still staying with his friend Rick?"

The threat hung in the air between us as the blood rushed from my face.

"Leave my brother alone..." I warned through clenched teeth.

"Or what?"

"Or I will kill you." I stormed out of the house shaking, my breathing coming in short, panicked gasps.

On the drive back to the Count's mansion, I struggled to calm myself, and as I passed a liquor store along the way, the temptation to stop nearly overwhelmed me.

It was so hard to avert my eyes from the bottles I saw lined up through the window. I had to remind myself a dozen times just why I've decided to remain sober. Alcohol was never my drug of choice, but it could serve in a pinch, hit that spot I needed, and it was sure a hell of a lot easier to acquire than what I really wanted. But no. I couldn't. I couldn't fall down that rabbit hole again.

I pressed the gas and reached for my water bottle instead. I didn't have time to get drunk, anyway. I had to concentrate on my plan, and I had only a month to make it all happen. The bastard.

Which meant I needed to keep my eyes peeled on how to get that key and the passcode. Then, I'd be free. Setting this up would make me right with that asshole and finally give me enough to get my brother out of there.

Failure was not an option.

When I arrived at the mansion, it was so quiet I wasn't sure anyone was home, so I decided to use the time to look around. Maybe I'd be lucky and find the key to the office, or a sheet of paper with the safe passcode. Ha! Either way, snooping around would give me a better sense of the space and security, and I could always justify, if I were caught, that I was simply scoping out my cleaning work for the night.

I started in the kitchen, this time checking every drawer and cupboard for any keys instead of food. My search turned up empty on the key front, but I did discover a box of chocolate chip cookies, so score.

I made my way through hallways next, poking into the many rooms as I passed them. Most were guest bedrooms that looked like they'd never been used.

I took my time, keeping my search careful and quiet. Honestly, I was terrified of accidentally walking in on the Count while he slept. Somehow, I didn't think he'd be pleased with that with all his comments about privacy.

But then, I could always say I was exploring and got lost, and since it wasn't entirely untrue, it wouldn't count as a lie.

As if semantics mattered at this point.

By the time I got to the third floor, I was pretty convinced I wouldn't find anything other than more bedrooms. There were a loooooottttt of freaking guest rooms. Who knew so many people that you'd need this many rooms all at once? It was astonishing.

So, I was definitely not expecting what I found when I opened the third door down the hall on the left.

At first glance, it looked nearly identical to every other room I'd opened.

The fireplace. The ornate furniture. The fancy four-poster bed.

It differed only in one detail.

This fancy bed had a woman's naked body lying on it.

or a moment, I thought she was dead. She looked so pale, so lifeless.

But then she moaned and opened her eyes, and I jumped back and let out a scream.

She sat up and her eyes widened when she saw me. "Who are you?" Then she shook her head and laughed. "Never mind, it doesn't matter. I've got to get going."

She rose from the bed, still totally naked, collected her clothing from various spots around the floor and dressed quickly.

"Any message you'd like me to pass on?" I asked as she pushed past me to get out.

She paused and looked me up and down. "Not

for him. But for you… if you have the chance, he's the best lay I've ever had. Highly recommend."

I stared at her, open-mouthed, and I tried to banish the thoughts her comment put into my head, but it was too late. I couldn't erase from my mind the fantasy of the Count and I together, naked, our bodies writhing as we pleasured each other.

She smiled like she could read my mind, then disappeared down the hall and down the stairs.

To take my mind off the Count, I decided to start my job a little early and began with tidying up the room that the woman had slept in.

It was hard to school my thoughts, and I kept vacillating from illicit fantasies of my own to wondering just why she'd stayed in a guest room instead of the Count's.

Finally, frustrated and bothered, I gave up searching the rest of the house and returned to my own room.

When evening arrived, Leonard gave me the tour of the cleaning supplies and then walked me through the various areas, starting with those to be cleaned daily, then on to those simply to be aired out and dusted less often. Fortunately, I wasn't expected to clean most of the bedrooms every day. That would've required a whole team of housekeepers, not just me.

The first time I cleaned the mansion, it took me over nine hours and by the end, I'd nearly rubbed my fingers raw.

My back ached and my cheek throbbed as I headed for the Count's room. Leonard had stressed I save his for last. And finally, the last it was. With a yawn, I knocked on the door, and when he didn't answer, I let myself in.

An immaculate room stretched out before me, one already so clean I wasn't sure what there was left to do other than maybe run a vacuum over the large oriental carpet. Perhaps, mop the exposed hardwood?

With echoes of my earlier fantasies threatening to parade once again in my head, I cast a quick eye at the bed. There weren't any naked women hiding in it, and the deep blue silk sheets and comforter were neatly folded, the bed expertly made. The windows were covered with black-out blinds that left the room void of any natural light, and since Leonard told me to leave those alone, so I did.

Strange how the Count didn't like windows or the sun. And just as strange that he slept during the day and kept the windows of the house locked down. But then, weren't the ultra-rich an odd lot, anyway?

I'd just finished dusting the dresser when I heard a

door open and turned around, nearly dropping my cleaning supplies in surprise.

It was the Count, standing there, totally naked, his body glistening from a recent shower or bath.

I knew I should look away, make apologies, or run and hide… Hell, maybe all three, but I couldn't take my eyes off of him. His body was a chiseled masterpiece of a sculpture, all hard angles, chorded muscles, and strong lines. God, what would it be like to touch him? Run my hands over those bands of abs? Feel every ripple of strength in him? Small wonder the woman I'd met had been so impressed with him. If he had the bedroom skills to match his looks… Yes, my eyes dropped down. I couldn't stop them.

Holy shit.

The Count cleared his throat. "I think this room is clean enough for now, Kassandra. Thank you."

I shook my head to clear my thoughts, though it didn't much help. "Sorry, yeah. I didn't know you were in here. I… didn't hear the shower."

"I was in the bath," he corrected.

"Right. Well, um. I'll leave you to it, then," I mumbled, turning to leave.

"I have company joining me soon," he called after me. "Please bring up refreshments when you are able."

"Will do," I said, closing the door behind me. Once out of his sight, I leaned against the wall to catch my breath, and then walked to the kitchen in a daze.

His eyes were so penetrating, like he could see straight into my soul. I crossed my arms over my chest and shivered at the thought. Then, I snorted. Hell, if he could see into my soul, I wouldn't be working here.

I tried to distract myself from the Count and his well-endowed assets, by preparing the refreshments he'd asked for. About ten minutes later, I heard Leonard greet someone at the door.

A tinkle of a laugh announced it was another woman.

As the butler escorted her upstairs, I squashed another flare of jealousy and searched for the wine bottle the Count last used. When I couldn't find it, I gave up and filled two cups with sparkling water instead, that and some fruit, cheese, and nuts and I was ready to take the tray upstairs.

Just as I lifted my hand to knock on the Count's bedroom door, I heard a moan.

I paused. Then, curious, I flattened my ear against the smooth, polished wood.

The sounds of sex—of really amazing sex—

created an instant reaction in my body. I shivered and pulled back then placed the tray by the door and turned to walk away.

But as I passed the bedroom next to the Count's, a bad idea leapt into my mind—a really very bad idea. But I couldn't stop myself. Quietly, I let myself in, and closed and locked the door behind me.

I could still hear them through the walls, maybe even better than in the hall. The grunting, the moaning, and the slapping of skin on skin. The woman gasped, her voice riddled with pleasure and the sound tipped me over the edge.

I dropped onto the bed and laid back, closing my eyes as I slid my hand beneath the waistband of my pants. I lost myself in the fantasy then, drowning in the imagined sensations of the Count's hands on my breasts, the feel of his body pressing against mine. It had been a long time since I'd had sex or enjoyed the feeling of someone touching me for pleasure—even if not love.

I stayed there, listening and writhing, and when the girl in the other room climaxed, I joined her quietly, my body releasing the pent frustration I'd been carrying for so long.

I didn't linger afterwards. I smoothed the bed

covers quickly and left before anyone could know I'd been there.

The warmth running through my body gave me a little lift as I finished my cleaning shift and grabbed dinner to take up to my room. The instant I sank down on my bed, I knew I wasn't getting up again for a good ten hours or more.

Even for so much money, cleaning this mansion was a shit ton of work. Something was going to have to give. I'd either have to get faster or I'd demand a different schedule. Maybe if the Count cut back on the women, I wouldn't have as much work to do.

That thought pleased me far more than it should have—the Count cutting back part, and annoyed with myself, I turned in the bed, preparing to sleep.

But even though my body ached and my hands hurt, sleep eluded me. I spent a few hours tossing and turning, until finally, I gave up and got ready for another day.

When I went downstairs, I found my cellphone on the table in the entryway, along with a key to the house and a note from the Count.

YOUR SERVICE LAST NIGHT WAS APPRECIATED.

Two weeks flew by in a flurry of routine and stolen glances of the Count as he escorted a new woman—sometimes two—into his room each night. And each night, I succumbed to my fantasies of him. How could I stop? He was beyond captivating, and a mystery.

The past few days, he'd taken to joining me in the kitchen at the end of my shift. I'd sit at the island, drinking tea as he drank his strange wine.

We didn't always talk. Sometimes, I'd work on a crossword puzzle and he'd help me when I got stuck. His vocabulary never failed to amaze me. I'd never met anyone with such a command of archaic words.

At other times, we'd each read a book, alone but together.

Still, through it all, I was counting the days I had left. And I kept my eyes peeled for a chance to borrow his keys so I could make a copy of the office one. But he never left them unattended, instead, he kept them in his pocket, so my chance never came.

The texts demanding updates were regular, and each morning, I dreaded getting my phone back. It was so hard to read the escalating threats. I'd spent more time than I liked placating Don while checking on Jeremy. Jeremy was having it rough, and each day my heart broke a little more for him.

God, I couldn't fail. I had to get him out of all this. He, at least, had to succeed, had to make something of himself. I couldn't let him follow my path. I just couldn't.

One night, the Count came down to the kitchen where I sat engrossed in a new novel while nibbling on an oatmeal cookie. He cleared his throat twice to secure my attention before I noticed him.

"Sorry," I apologized.

"Tomorrow evening I wish not to be disturbed by anything," he informed me in a distant tone. "You will have the evening off to do as you wish."

I wanted to ask him what was up, but I knew him well enough to read his expression, one that definitely did *not* invite inquiries, so I nodded and returned to my book.

The Count stood there a moment, inhaling deeply, but as he turned to leave the kitchen, he paused and raised a quizzical brow. "Have you been injured?" he asked unexpectedly.

I blinked, confused. "No?"

His eyes turned into slits. "You haven't had a cut or been bleeding of late?"

I felt the color rise on my cheeks. The razor, the

cut, the blood, the release, right before I'd come down for tea. "I nicked myself shaving," I said. Technically, it wasn't a lie. "But it's nothing big."

He stood there, just watching me for a good ten seconds, and then he nodded once and left.

I shivered, a little creeped out. How the *hell* had he smelled my blood?

After assuring myself I was truly alone, I pulled back my robe and examined my thigh, running a finger over the thin white lines. The pattern of them soothed me in a sick and twisted kind of way, and my eyes began to burn with tears as I considered just how messed up I was. Jeremy deserved so much better than what I was giving him. But I was his best shot at getting out of his screwed-up hellhole of a life to make something of himself, and I wouldn't fail.

With a sigh, I retied my robe and returned to my book.

A few minutes later, Leonard came into the kitchen, dressed not for bed for but travel.

"Are you going somewhere?" I asked, eying his smart jacket and stuffed duffle bag. Wherever he was going, it was for longer than one night.

"The Count has sent me on an errand," he replied. "I'll be gone for at least a fortnight. Will you need anything before I go?"

"No," I shook my head and grinned. "I think I've got the hang of things."

"Then, good evening."

"Safe travels." I said, rising to shake his hand.

After he left, I settled back onto the stool, feeling a bit strange knowing I'd be alone in the house with the Count for so long. Well, other than his rotating door of women, that was... Women who always left looking quite satisfied.

Each day, I struggled a bit more with the jealousy as well as the thoughts, the curiosity of just what the Count did in bed. God, what would it be like to be the center of his attention? No other man I'd ever met could even come close to his natural sexiness and charisma. The charm oozed off him so easily.

If only...

I scowl, irritated to find myself succumbing to such thoughts once again. I sure as hell couldn't initiate a relationship with my boss. That was just generally a bad idea. And doubly one when you're trying to rob him. Yeah, I didn't know a lot about love or romance, but even I knew that wasn't how it was supposed to go.

Feeling frustrated, I left the kitchen and made my way into the media room. It was a virtual theater, complete with the most comfortable reclining chairs and a giant screen hanging on the wall for watching movies. A bar sat in the corner, but I knew it no longer stocked alcohol. I'd checked. Several times. Each time after I'd texted Don.

Still, I came to this room often and for a different reason. I came trying to find answers to the past, but no answers were forthcoming.

"Would you care to watch something?"

I spun around to find the Count standing there, studying me with his magnetic dark gaze.

"No, um. I was just… " I fumbled for words. Then, I blurted, "Did you know someone was murdered in this house?"

He tilted his head. "Yes, I'm quite aware."

I stared at him, astonished. "And that doesn't bother you?"

He responded with a casual shrug. "No. Death has never been a particular worry of mine. And as for violence, I'm fairly impervious." He entered the room and took a seat in one of the chairs to stretch out his long, elegant legs. "Does it bother you?" he asked with a curious lift of his brow.

It did. A lot. I took the liberty of sitting in the chair to his right as I confessed, "I was here. The night it happened."

That surprised him. I could tell by the way his

eyes widened. "And yet you chose to work here? Why?"

"Maybe I'm impervious to violence, as well," I replied. That was a lie. I attracted violence like a magnet. But I was a survivor. I turned my head to the side and added in a low voice. "When you grow up the way I did, you get used to anything, I suppose."

You did. And especially with dark things. A lot of shit went down that night. Death was just part of it.

Silence fell, but strangely, I wasn't tempted to start filling it with babble. We just sat there, companionably.

Then, after a time, the Count stirred. "Shall we watch a movie?"

"A movie?"

Amusement glinted in his dark eyes. "You are familiar with the concept, I assume?"

I laughed and leaned back in my plush chair, feeling strangely lighthearted. "Yes, I'm familiar. What did you have in mind?"

He clicked the remote and scrolled through titles. "How about Dracula?"

I grinned. "Old school. I like it."

He scowled at me. "Not that old."

But I didn't have time to dissect his reaction

anymore as he dimmed the lights with the remote and the movie started.

I'd be lying if I said I watched the movie. Well, I scanned the screen from time to time and pretended to follow the plot, but my attention was on the Count more than anything else. It was impossible to sit so close without being keenly aware of his every move. From time to time, our fingers accidentally brushed against each other, his leg would shift, or our feet would touch.

Finally, when the film ended, he stood. "Thank you for indulging me. Now, I shall retire."

I glanced at the clock. 9:40p.m. Strange. The Count was usually in bed with a woman by now, having gone at it for at least a few hours.

"You don't have a date tonight?" I asked, the surprise having loosened my tongue, but who could blame me? It was the first night since I started working here that he wasn't entertaining a woman.

"Not tonight. Have a good day, Kassandra. And rest well."

I watched him walk out and then stretched in preparation of my nightly duties. I had an easy schedule for tonight, just the—

My eyes fell on the bar counter. Something glistened in the light.

Were those…keys?

I was there in an instant. My. God. *Keys*. He'd left them there, next to the remote. His fucking key chain and on it, the key to his *study*.

I swallowed as my fingers trembled with excitement.

The hardware store closed at 11:00p.m. If I hurried, I could make it there, copy the key and the return before I got caught, and it all went to shit.

I didn't stop to think twice. I grabbed the keys and flew to my room, snagged my purse and shrugged into a sweatshirt as I hurried down the stairs. Minutes later, I was speeding down the road, I was halfway into town before I realized the reason I couldn't see so well was because I'd forgotten to switch on the headlights.

Chill, Kass. Getting a ticket right now will only make things worse. Yeah, I'd have to break into the hardware store to make the copy, then, and add that to my list of crimes.

I make it inside the store and in minutes, I'm out again, my copy of the key lying cool in my palm. I freaking did it. Step One. I had the office key, safe and secure.

I grinned and closed my eyes. *Halfway there, baby. Jeremy, we're halfway there.*

Giddy with relief, I zoomed back to the mansion —this time, with headlights on—and I was practically dancing the two-step as I stepped through the front door. I pulled out the Count's keys from my purse and gripped them tightly to keep them from jingling.

Now, the only thing left was to return the keys back to the—

The shadows to my left shifted.

Shit.

It was the Count.

5

"You have returned?" the Count's deep baritone slid over my skin like a caress even as my heart threatened to burst from sheer panic. "Where did you go, Kassandra?"

The rule. I couldn't lie to him. I swallowed and licked my dry lips. "It's a surprise." It was. A bad one.

"Surprise?"

"Yep." I forced my lips into a smile and gripped the keys tighter, willing them with all my might to not make a sound, not one freaking sound.

"And what surprise is that?"

"If I tell you, it wouldn't be a surprise then, would it?" I challenged, my nerves standing on edge. And as far as surprises went, trust me, he really didn't want to know about this one.

"I'm not keen on surprises, Miss Blackwood." The disapproval hung heavy in his voice.

So, I was Miss Blackwood all of a sudden? What happened to Kassandra? Did that mean something…bad?

He stepped closer, looming over me in the darkness less than an arm's length away. His eyes seemed to glint as they searched mine.

Every cell in me wanted to run, but I couldn't. I stood there, pinned by his gaze like a deer caught in headlights. After several attempts at clearing my throat, I rasped, "Can I get you something, Sir?"

I winced. Since when had I ever called him 'sir?' God, I sucked at being a criminal.

It was dark, but the moonlight was bright enough to allow me to see the suspicion that marched over his face.

"Must I remind you of the rules, Miss Blackwood?"

"Yeah, I know them. Don't lie, steal, or disobey." A bead of sweat trickled down my cheek.

"Then, do not disobey me. Tell me of your surprise."

Well, this was great. He had me fenced in here. My thoughts whirled through various possibilities, but I couldn't think of any combinations that would get me out of my predicament this time.

Real fear stabbed through me as I bit the corner of my lip in thought, accidentally biting a little too hard in the process. Shit. I winced a little as my mouth filled with the coppery tang of blood.

The Count sucked in a long breath.

Yeah, I'm thinking. Think, Kass. Think.

Deep inside, I hated betraying him like this.

Hated lying.

Hated that I had a life that required such things in order to survive.

Then, he was there, standing right in front of me only inches away, his enigmatic gaze locked on my mouth.

All thoughts of keys flew out the window and all I could think about was how much I wanted—needed—his mouth on mine, his body on mine. God, what would his lips feel like? Just once, I'd like to kiss him, if only to see if he lived up to my fantasies. Something told me he would. No, he'd exceed them, surely.

Then, as if he'd read my thoughts, I felt his hands cupping my face. Gently, he tilted my chin up as he leaned down, angling my mouth closer to his. I felt his breath on my lips and this close, his eyes seem wider, wilder even, but perhaps that was just a trick of the moonlight and shadows.

Slowly, ever so slowly, he closed the distance between us until, at last, our lips met.

Nothing could have prepared me for the way his mouth took mine. Raw power and primal need mixed with a surprising tenderness.

His tongue danced over my lips and into my mouth with an expertise that left me weak-kneed and melting against his hard chest, helpless to the sensations he sent rocketing through my body.

No wonder there was an endless revolving door of women to this place.

If this was his kiss, just what was he like in bed?

Then, when I was sure this moment couldn't get any better, he crushed me close and sucked my entire lower lip into his mouth, drawing upon it so deeply I tasted my own blood as he drew me in.

God, I didn't know you could have an orgasm from a kiss alone, but I was so close. I was on the precipice of a cliff, dangling off the edge as I clung desperately to him in.

His arms embraced me, one hand sliding to the dip in my lower back, pressing our hips together, the other hand trailing down my spine.

My legs quivered as I came in his arms, deep pleasure crashing over me like waves.

As if from miles away, I heard the keys fall to the floor.

Then, he pulled away and lifted his head, leaving me feeling bereft. Lost. And the next instant, he was gone, vanishing into the darkness.

I drew a shaky breath wanting to run after him. I actually took a step forward, but then, my foot collided with the keys to send them skittering across the marble floor.

Shit.

Shit. Shit. Shit. Shit.

My heart stood still, numb with horror.

So close. I'd almost lost it all over a kiss—but what a kiss—*No, Kass. Kissing your boss won't end well.*

Especially when he could have caught you with his keys.

Panicking, I snatched the keys from the floor and ran through the halls like a madwoman, back to the media room. In three seconds flat, I'd dropped the keys on the bar and then I was back in the hall, running to my own room.

Once inside, I slammed the door shut and leaned against the wood, shaking.

It took me longer than I cared to admit before I felt strong enough to stumble to my bed. I knew I should be working. I had rooms to clean, rugs to vacuum, and laundry to wash, but I couldn't move, not with the strength of the fear and pleasure running riot in my head.

It must have been nearly an hour later before I recovered my composure to venture outside the door once again.

I set about my nightly tasks, nervous and on edge. Just what would I say to the Count should he appear again?

And had he seen the keys?

Finally, I saw the gray light of dawn that signaled the end of my shift and I stumbled back to room, exhausted.

I hadn't seen hide nor hair of the Count. And exactly how I felt about that, I couldn't say beyond part of me was relieved and the other, devastated.

After taking a long, hot shower and after verifying for the tenth time that my copy of the key was safely tucked away, I finally dropped myself into bed and allowed my eyes to drift shut.

I AWOKE TO THE WARM RAYS OF THE SUN ON MY

face. For a minute, I just stared at the ceiling in a kind of peaceful daze.

Then, I remembered the key.

I sat bolt upright.

The key. I'd done it. I'd gotten the damn key. Step One of the plan was complete.

Then, I recalled the kiss. Slowly, I ran a fingertip over my lips. With the strength with which the Count had sucked on my lower lip, I'd have expected it to feel sore, tender, but it didn't.

Had it been a dream?

No. It couldn't have been.

Yet... how could a mere kiss have pulled such feelings from me? Had I been so desperate, so lonely, that I'd overreacted to such an extent?

Yeah, that made more sense, knowing me.

With a snort, I rolled out of bed, dressed and headed downstairs to the kitchen. I needed coffee. Badly.

But the instant I shoved open the doors, my heart froze.

Don.

Just sitting there at the island, tapping his fingers on the granite.

"Strange, isn't it, just how empty this place is during the day?" he asked in a conversational tone.

"How did you get in?" I asked.

"Someone was careless," he said. "The front door was unlocked."

I felt sick with the realization that I had done that. I had left it unlocked when I came back last night. The kiss had distracted me. Leonard was gone.

This was my fault.

I drew a shaky breath and then pointed to the door. "Out," I choked. "You can't be here."

"Well, now, if you answered my texts I wouldn't have to come now, would I, Kass?" he asked, jabbing his finger onto the granite with every word. "You're two weeks into your month and I've heard nothing. Nothing. You've got to give me something."

I thinned my lips and scowled. "I got something, but I'm not talking about it here."

"Oh?"

"Yes," I spat. "Get out and I'll give it to you."

"Meet me on the road. Ten minutes."

He left then, but not before going out of his way to brush himself against me in his typical power play.

I ran back to my room and grabbed the key with shaking fingers. Part of me is relieved to be rid of it. No key. No evidence of my betrayal.

"Didn't think you'd show," Don greeted me as I stepped out of my car on the side of a dirt road.

"I told you, I'm good for it," I replied, marching over to slam the key in his outstretched palm. "The key to the office."

He grinned and then held the key up to the sunlight, as if an inspection alone could prove it genuine. "You know what this means, Kassy?"

"That you should get out of my hair?" I asked in a waspish tone.

"No," he chuckled. He bent down to plant his face in mine. "This means you've got more in you than you're admitting." He pulled back and brandished the key in my face. "I'm not waiting another two weeks for the passcode. Now, you've got only a week."

I froze, finding it hard to even breathe. "You can't do this."

"Oh, I can, and I am," he retorted. He chucked me under the chin and then opened the door of his car, but before sliding inside, he paused to add "Remember, Jeremy will want you to do your best, now."

I stood there, unable to move.

I couldn't fail, I knew that, but now? Now, how can I possibly succeed?

6

J couldn't stop shaking. Don left and I sat in my car, engine idling, hands on the steering wheel, my heart racing so fast in my chest I legit started worrying about a heart attack. Even the bright day surrounding me seemed oppressive, as if choking me so I couldn't breathe.

I don't remember driving back to the mansion or getting to my bedroom. I do remember pulling out my small box of supplies and sitting in front of the fire with it. I remember staring at my distorted reflection in the tiny razor blade. I remember pressing it to my thigh and feeling all the stress and pain and anxiety bleed out. I remember the release. Then, the shame and guilt.

There had to be a better way of dealing with my

tortured soul. But I had yet to find one, and honestly, my life was in such a shitty place did it really matter? Wasn't this the least of my worries?

After I cleaned myself up, I crawled into bed and tried to sleep, but regret wormed its way into me. I hated betraying the Count, when he'd been nothing but kind to me. Not to mention generous.

I hated helping Don, but how else could I get out from under his oppressive thumb that turned to a dangerous fist at the first sign of challenge? In the end, it was my own damn fault for getting so deep into the drug scene, for owing him so much money. That and the fact he was the only one I knew who could get my brother and I fake IDs to start a new life away from this hell hole... I had no choice.

Right?

Yeah, Don was a master at dangling what you needed in front of you, and if that didn't work, following it up with what you feared the most if you didn't deliver.

I needed Jeremy to be safe. And that was exactly what Don dangled and threatened me with.

I'd do anything for my brother.

I tossed and turned, and when the sun rose high enough in the sky, I had to use my sun-blocking curtains to get any sleep at all.

After everything that had occurred, I'd thought I would have had nightmares, but instead I dreamed of the Count, of his lips on mine, his hands running over my body, of him doing to me what he did to all those other women who left looking so smugly satisfied. I woke so horny I was already halfway to an orgasm, so I closed my eyes and pretended my fingers were the Count's and used my imagination to finish myself off.

Nothing like starting the day desperate to shag your boss. I cringed at the thought of meeting him again, considering the last time we'd been together he'd kissed me into an orgasm. Just how do you look your boss in the eye after that?

In the end, I only managed about four hours of sleep before I gave up entirely. There was, after all, plenty of daylight left before I needed to start my shift.

I decided to surprise Jeremy with a trip for ice cream. I needed to make sure he was okay and had a safe place to stay. As hard as all this was for me, it was so much worse for him. He'd been closer to our mother, and she'd protected him as best she could from our father's temper. Without her, Jeremy's life had fallen apart.

I grabbed my keys and headed for the front door.

The scuff of my every tiptoed step and the slight jingling of the keys sounded so loud in the unnatural silence. How could the Count sleep like the dead during the day? But then, it matched. He kept his house as cold and silent as a tomb.

My car was the only thing that didn't fit in this pristine glamour of wealth that surrounded me. It sat in the corner of the driveway like a wart on a model's face—entirely out of place. It took a few tries before the old beast coughed to life, sounding like a long-time smoker on its last breath.

I pulled up to Jeremy's school just before the final bell, and his face lit up when he saw my beat-up Subaru in the pick-up line.

He climbed into the front seat, filling the car with the smell of sweaty teenage boy. "I didn't know you were coming today," he said, grinning from ear to ear.

"I wanted to surprise you. Ice cream or froyo?" I asked, though I already knew the answer.

"Ice cream!"

We made it to the ice cream parlor in under three minutes, and after we'd seated ourselves on a pair heart-shaped, wrought iron chairs in the back with our decadent treats, Jeremy told me about his day.

"I got the highest grade in my class on our bio test this week," he said with pride. "My teacher wants me to participate in the science fair this year." Then, his face dropped. "There's a fee to enter though, and the materials cost money, so I told her I couldn't."

"I can get the money," I said.

He shrugged. "Where would I work on it? Where would I store it?"

All good questions. Home was out of the question.

"Where are you staying?" I asked.

"I'm still at Rick's house, but I can't stay much longer. His parents are starting to ask questions. I tried renting a room at a motel, but I need an adult to sign in," he said.

"I'll go with you to take care of that today," I said. "And look, my plan is coming together. I'll get us out of here. I swear it."

He nodded, eyes glossy with emotion. "I believe you," he whispered.

Once we'd finished our ice cream, I took him to the store to pick up some Chef Boyardee, canned beef stew, and bananas, and then rented a motel room for the week at the Windmill Hotel. The place had obviously seen better days, but at least it wasn't one of those pay-by-the-hour joints.

"It's not bad," I repeated for the third time, eyeing the dingy, lumpy floors, peeling wallpaper, and

the faded comforter. The TV worked, all three chan-
nels. As shabby as it was, I knew I couldn't afford
even that long term. "Don't tell anyone you're staying
here," I reminded him.

Jeremy rolled his eyes. "I'm not stupid."

I ruffled his hair. "I know you're not, but we can't
be too careful right now. Also, when you walk to and
from school—and anywhere else, make sure you're
not followed, okay? Do you remember what I taught
you about that?"

He nodded. "Never take the same route at the
same time. Check behind you frequently. Take paths
that cars can't go down. Go into stores if you need to
ditch someone."

"You're a smart kid," I said, then kissed him on
the forehead. "I have to go. Get your homework done
and stay inside tonight."

He looked so sad when I left that I felt my heart
break.

THE SUN HAD JUST DIPPED BELOW THE HORIZON
when I arrived back at the mansion. As I rushed to
start my shift, I spied the Count roaming the second
floor, looking lost and fragile and very unlike his
normal self. Any cringeworthy thoughts I'd had fled

out the window as again, my heart melted. First Jeremy, now the Count?

I actually took a step in the Count's direction before I heard his deep baritone from yesterday, playing in my mind, *"Tomorrow evening I wish not to be disturbed by anything."*

Well, 'anything' included me, didn't it? Deciding to play it safe, I left him to wander in his forlorn fashion and threw myself into my work.

In my short time as a housekeeper, I'd found cleaning therapeutic, a good physical exercise that generally let me lose myself in the task at hand for a few hours.

But not today.

With Jeremy safe and sound, for now, my mind ricocheted back to Don and his escalation of the timeline. Seven days. Jerk. With only a week left to figure out the safe's code, I'd have to move fast. I marched around the house, mopping floors, vacuuming curtains, and dusting bookshelves—man, I'd never seen so many books, and such old ones, crammed in every room—all the while, mulling over just how I might get Don's blasted code to the safe. I didn't let myself dwell on exactly what would happen after he got it. If I did, I just might not carry through, and I couldn't risk that. Jeremy was counting on me.

Several hours into my shift, a loud banging on the front door shattered my thoughts. I hurried to a window and craned my neck for a view, but the angles were wrong, and shadows shrouded what little I could see.

Then, I heard my name, even through the glass. "*Kassandra*. Kassssandra!"

My stomach dropped.

Shit.

Double shit.

And tonight of all nights? The night the Count made it very clear he didn't want disturbances of any kind?

Steeling myself for an unpleasant confrontation, I stormed to the front door and pulled it open.

My drunk father lost his balance and fell back a few steps.

"*There* you are, you little slut." He glared at me from bleary, bloodshot eyes. "Whoring yourself again, are you?"

He grabbed my arm, yanked me towards him, and then slammed me into one of the rose bushes.

"What the hell are you doing here?" I hissed as I righted myself and began pulling thorns out of my skin.

"Coming to collect what's mine. Where's that brat of a brother of yours?"

"Not here," I snapped. "And not where you can find him. Now get the hell out of here before I call the cops."

He laughed, a twisted humorless sound bathed in liquor and hatred. "Go ahead, call them. I think Jerry's on duty tonight. We had drinks just last week. I'll tell him all about how you kidnapped my son. A minor. How will that go, do you think, given your record? I have a right to my boy."

I shoved him away, but his height and bulk gave him an advantage and he raised his fist and slammed it into my face before I could dodge him.

I fell back into the bushes, crushing the flowers and feeling the bite of the thorns once again. Blood coated my mouth, and I flicked my tongue against the split in my lip.

I stood up, my head spinning, my anger boiling. "Leave us alone!"

He body-rushed me, pinning me against the wall, his meaty arm tucked under my chin and crushing my throat until I couldn't breathe.

"You'll bring my boy back or they won't find your body, not that anyone would bother looking!"

I could feel my consciousness fading, but before it

did, I managed to lift my leg and ram my knee into his groin.

He released me and fell back, screaming in pain as I slumped to the ground choking and holding my throat.

That's when the Count walked through the front door.

"I asked for quiet!" he began imperiously. Then, catching sight of my father, he cocked a slow brow at him. "Who are you and why are you on my property?"

"That's my father," I whispered, my throat already swelling. "I told him to leave. I'm sorry."

Always. Freaking. Apologizing. For my shit of a family.

Then the Count marched to my father, leaned over and lifted him by the collar of his shirt, straight into the air. I gaped. While the Count stood taller than my father, he wasn't bulkier. Yet, he lifted my father as if he weighed no more than a feather.

"Get off my property and keep your hands off my staff or it's your body that won't be found," the Count said, speaking every word with a slow deliberate calm that sent shivers up my spine.

My father quailed in his boots and then made a mad dash back to his car. The next minute, he peeled away, down the private road and probably to the nearest bar.

With him gone, I tried to stand, but a wave of dizziness struck, and I nearly toppled over.

Strong hands caught and steadied me. Then, the Count lifted me into his arms as if I weighed no more than a child and carried me into his house.

As he walked up the stairs toward his private suite, I let my head fall against his chest. I felt numb. Overwhelmed. I didn't want to think anymore, so I didn't. I just rested my head, wanting nothing more than to hear the solid beating of the chest beneath my ear.

Only…there was nothing. Not a single heartbeat, no matter how much I strained to hear. Maybe it was the pounding in my own head, drowning out everything else?

The Count placed me on his bed and stoked the fire, and then left, only to return a moment later with a glass of something dark and red. "This will help you heal," he said, handing me the cup. "It's an old family recipe."

He stood over me, so cold and distant, yet the arm he slid behind my back was the gentlest I'd ever felt as he helped me sit up to drink.

The metallic, bitter taste combined with the pain

in my sore throat nearly made me gag, but I forced myself to drink the entire concoction, and then handed him back the cup.

"What was in that?" I asked as he carefully eased me back down on the pillows.

"A special brew," he answered. "Herbs from my homeland and a few other things you wouldn't be able to find here."

A warmth began spreading through me, making me feel almost drunk. The thought made me panic. Had I just accidentally blown my sobriety after working so damn hard for over a year? I shot up in the bed, my heart pounding, but the sudden movement made me clutch my head in instant regret.

"Rest," the Count's deep baritone urged.

"Am I drunk?" I groaned. "Was there something in that?"

"No. You have a concussion and some bleeding. The drink will help, and you might feel different for a time, but I did not drug you. On that, I give you my word. Now, rest."

His words held such command that I couldn't resist them, and almost immediately, I fell back into the bed and into a deep sleep.

When I woke next, it was to find the Count sitting in front of a crackling fire, nursing what looked like a tumbler of whiskey. He shifted at once, apparently sensing the instant I'd opened my eyes.

"Why was your father here?" he asked, staring at the flames dancing on the logs.

My father. I didn't really want to talk about him. Swallowing a sigh, I climbed out of the bed, preparing to wince in pain, but instead, to my surprise, I felt only a small twinge. I flexed my jaw in wonder, marveling at my speedy recovery. I'd expected to feel that beating for weeks.

Then, I recalled the Count's question and joined him at the fireplace. "He was looking for my brother," I said.

The Count waved me to the tufted leather chair opposite him, and after I'd taken my seat, looked over to me with dark penetrating eyes. "And where is your brother?"

"Safe," I said defensively. "Well, safe enough, I hope." And that was all he was going to learn about Jeremy. "I'm sorry for bothering you tonight," I said, switching the subject, "But, thank you for your help."

He graced me with a curt nod and returned his gaze to the fire. "Don't let your personal life get in the way again," he said.

Stung by his sudden harshness, I rose to my feet. "I won't," I replied, turning to leave.

But he began speaking before I could get far. "Tonight is my wedding anniversary."

That paused me. "You're...married?" With that long parade of women?

"I was," he murmured, his gaze once again locked on the fire. "She died."

I hesitated. Was he opening up? When he didn't continue, I inched back to the leather chair, sat, and waited.

"She was murdered," he said at last, his face a hardened mask. "She was pregnant at the time."

"Shit." I swallowed. That had to be rough. "I'm so sorry."

He took a drink. "The baby wasn't mine. Though, I did think he was until after her death. I'd always wanted a child of my own." He drew a long breath, and then added, "I cannot imagine the depravity of someone who would abuse such a gift."

I looked away from him, his grief and my own pain mixing in my soul to create a cocktail of despair I couldn't stomach. I had no words of comfort to offer him. I had none for myself, either. We were both broken spirits trying to make the best of the hands we'd been dealt.

"My mother died in an 'accident'," I offered when

the silence had dragged on too long. "But I know my father killed her in one of his rages."

The Count gave a solemn nod. "The authorities didn't investigate?"

I scoffed. "My dad was a cop. He was the *'authorities'* in this town." Which is why, though I threatened to call the cops on him many times, he and I both knew it was an idle threat. He didn't want his buddies seeing what he'd become, but he knew they wouldn't do anything to him.

The Count looked at me fully then, his face impassive. "Sometimes, we must make our own justice in this life."

I couldn't tell him then how right he was, but I wished I could have apologized. For what had happened to him because of his wife…and what was about to happen to him because of me.

*a*t the Count's insistence I rest, I returned to my room and plopped myself on my bed. Normally, I'd worry about my father returning, but after coming across someone capable of suspending him in the air like a ragdoll, I figured he wouldn't be so keen on a repeat. He didn't like looking like a fool, and dangling in the air had fool written all over it.

With my father out of the way—for now—I just had to worry about Don…but the instant I thought his name, I felt the weight of my own sins claw into my shoulders.

"For Jeremy," I whispered, forcing my thoughts to my brother's bright future. I'd make sure he succeeded. He'd enter that science fair and show them all what he was made of, just what he could become. I wouldn't let our family name, or my weaknesses, ruin his chances.

I rolled over and buried my face in my pillow, struggling to fight off the darkness gathering in my soul like a foul storm.

Shit. At this rate, I'd never be able to sleep again.

But as with all things, time won out and my body gave into its own exhaustion.

I woke with the shrouds of a nightmare clinging to my mind like a spider's web. Only I wasn't the spider in this scenario, I was the bug trapped for dinner.

Panic seized me at the memory of my father showing up, and of the ticking bomb I was living under. Six days.

Six days or he would hurt—maybe kill—Jeremy.

Six days to save him.

I grit my teeth and swung my legs out of bed. The angle of the sun streaming through the curtains told me I'd slept the morning away. It had to be early afternoon.

After a quick shower and a fresh change of clothes, I padded to the kitchen to make my breakfast. There wasn't much in the way of food, but I

KARPOV KINRADE & LIV CHATHAM

wasn't exactly hungry. I opted for a simple blended fruit shake of blueberries, milk, and ice. As I downed the drink, I couldn't help but recall the Count didn't seem to be a big eater. In fact, he seemed to drink a lot of liquid, especially his unusually thick, red wine.

"Focus, Kass," I grumbled at myself.

I had only six days left to get the code. I'd wasted yesterday. I couldn't afford to waste another day.

And now with the Count asleep, I had a good few hours to implement my plan…whatever that ended up being.

I sat down to drum my fingers on the kitchen table.

Right. Time to get cracking.

The code.

How was I supposed to get it?

Since I couldn't really hover over the Count's shoulder and take notes—without raising suspicion, anyway—the only option I had would be to record him when I wasn't around.

I'd heard one of Jeremy's teachers complaining about getting their ID stolen during a Mexican cruise. She'd bopped off the ship just long enough to buy some rum at the port, and when she hadn't had enough money, she'd used a nearby ATM to grab the cash. She'd returned home to phone calls from her

96

bank, asking if she was shopping in Brazil. She'd been the victim of a 'key skimmer', she'd called it.

Needing my phone and some fresh air, I retrieved it from the entry table where the Count had taken to leaving it and went outside to walk the gardens and research.

The late afternoon sun felt warm on my face as I typed in 'key skimmer.'

After clicking the first few links, I knew already I was in over my head. I couldn't even begin to fathom installing something like that on the Count's safe. Yeah, I'd made a lot of bad decisions in life, but I wasn't the full-fledged criminal required to pull off such a stunt. At least not yet, anyway.

No, I was more on the Teddy Bear cam level…

The thought of the enigmatic and imperious Count opening his door to see a Teddy Bear staring back at him made me grin.

Still, the more I thought about it, the more the idea stuck. Not the Teddy Bear part, of course, but the camera.

Leaning against a tall stately oak at the back of the garden I keyed a quick search of "mini spy cameras", and seconds later, I was in business. They even had them at Best Buy. It was still early in the day. I could pick one up, return, and then creep into the room to install it before the Count even budged from bed. Then, when he opened the safe within the next six days, voila, I'd have the code. Yes…he *would* open the safe in the next six days. He had to.

I winced. It was a fragile plan, at best… Yeah, I definitely wasn't criminally inclined… Oh, shit. *Shit.*

Don had the key.

I dropped my head back to bang it rhythmically against the tree trunk.

I had no choice. I'd have to ask for it back.

Much rather wanting to yank my own teeth out, I swallowed the bile rising in my throat and texted Don.

NEED THE KEY. MEET ME AT BEST BUY.

THE LITTLE DOTS POPPED UP AT ONCE, THE ONES showing he was texting a reply. I waited.

And waited.

Shit. He was typing a novel. This had to be bad. Why had I ever gotten involved with such a jerk to begin with?

Finally, his reply popped onto my screen.

. . .

6

I glared. He could go jump off a cliff. And into a pool of piranhas. Ignoring my phone, I headed to my car and left the property.

I didn't let myself think as I drove to town. Actually, I was getting pretty good at the not thinking bit. I just focused on the road, the blue sky, the trees waving in the light breeze.

As I navigated the parking lot and backed into my spot, I did let my thoughts wander back to the Count. In a secret, decadent way. Like when you indulge yourself with a real treat, creeping down to the fridge at night to pinch off a piece of that chocolate cake. You close your eyes, eat it, and moan as you lick the frosting on your fingers. I could think of a lot of scenarios with the Count that involved moaning and licking…

Catching the nature of my thoughts, I slammed on the brakes and switched off the engine.

"Get a grip, Kass," I muttered under my breath.

The Count was going to hate me soon enough. There'd be no licking and moaning in our future.

I hurried into the store. They had a few different mini models, one in a pen, one in a tiny cube, and one that looked like it was just stuck on a piece of Velcro. I bought all three. One of them would have to work.

I'd just closed my car door and reached for my phone to see where Don was when a hand pounded the window and I nearly jumped out of my skin.

"Six," Don mouthed as he leered at me through the glass.

How I wished I didn't have to roll the window down and talk to him. If only I could just floor the gas pedal and tear out of there, preferably running over his feet along the way.

But I couldn't. Clenching my jaw, I rolled the window down a few inches. "The key?" I demanded.

"Six," he said as he dropped the key in my lap.

"Yeah, got the message. Loud and clear. Six. Now, I've got to get back."

"You're not hearing me, Kass." He gripped the edge of the window with his fingers and leaned down to grin at me through the crack. It wasn't a nice grin. "I think you need a reminder."

"Not really," I disagreed. I revved the engine. I needed to get back. Now. Pronto. There weren't that many hours left before the Count woke up, and I had to get the cameras installed today if I had a prayer of making the deadline. "Gotta go, Don. I'm pressed for time."

"Those who don't listen pay a price," he said. He straightened, stretched, and then moved to the back of my car, saying, "We wouldn't want Jeremy to pay now, would we?"

I rolled the window down the rest of the way and leaned out. "Keep Jeremy out of this. You know the deal."

He bent over as if inspecting my rear wheel. I saw the flash, but I didn't understand until he turned, and I saw the knife in his hand.

"What the—"

I shot out of the car, shocked.

My tire. My freaking tire. He'd sliced it.

He grabbed my arm and drew me up close. "Wouldn't want that to be Jeremy now, would we?"

I didn't really need to hear that. I already knew what was at stake. I didn't need the mental images he was putting into my head. I replaced them with visions of my own, of Don's head on a silver platter.

Then, he let me go and stalked away.

At first, I couldn't move. I just leaned against the car to keep my knees from buckling.

Then, the sight of the flat tire brought me back to reality and anger chased out the fear.

I didn't have time for this. Or money. Or a god damned spare.

Why? *Why?*

Just what had I done to the universe to deserve this? I mean, once you've decided to get on the straight and narrow, that's when all the real problems and roadblocks spring in your way. Why did it have to be so damn hard? I was just trying to give Jeremy a better life. Surely, the universe could freaking respect that and just help out a little instead of putting Don constantly in my way?

With mounting fury, I drove my car two blocks to the tire store. Yeah, I know you're not supposed to drive on a flat, especially this flat of a flat, but what choice did I have?

"I need a tire patched," I told the guy that approached me with a well-practiced customer service smile on his freckled face.

He took one look at my tire and the smile vanished. "Sorry, lady, but this isn't a patch job. You need a new tire. Which means four new ones if you want the tread to wear right."

My irritation grew to epic levels. I was losing precious time. As it was, I'd be lucky to squeeze in a few minutes to hide the camera before the Count was out and about.

"Fine."

As I waited, I prepped for my mission, removing the camera packaging and tossing it in the trash so I wouldn't accidentally leave any evidence around.

Finally, four new tires later, I was racing back to the Count's house, fingers crossed my speed wouldn't attract any cops. This time, the universe showed a little pity, and I arrived back at the mansion with no cop the wiser.

Key and cameras in hand, I ran into the mansion and to the Count's office. According to my calculations, I had about fifteen minutes to set up and hide my surveillance system. I couldn't risk waiting another day. I was already down to six.

The key fit the lock perfectly and with a click, I was inside. The room was dark and as he didn't have any conventional lighting in his office--or even a freaking window--I had to let my eyes adjust until I could see well enough to place the cameras. It was just a matter of picking out which bookshelves provided the best angles of the safe.

I tucked the key into my shoe so I wouldn't accidentally leave it somewhere obvious, and then found hiding places for the first two cameras easily enough. I regretted my purchase of the pen version. It stuck out like a sore thumb and drew attention, practically advertising "look here."

I'd just removed it from the fourth location when the door to the study opened.

It was the Count.

8

The Count stood in the doorway with his dark eyes riveted on mine. "What are you doing in here?"

"Oh, just getting an early start to the cleaning," I squeaked and licked my dry lips.

His eyes flicked down to my mouth. A muscle tensed on his lean jaw. "This room is off limits."

"Oh?" I feigned surprise. "The door was open." Technically, not a lie. It was open...after I'd unlocked it.

He approached me slowly, like a predator hunting prey. "Do you remember the rules?" he whispered, towering over me. "Do not lie?"

"Yep. Rule number one, isn't it?" I smiled.

He loomed closer, and then closer still until I

could feel his breath on my face, and so help me, in spite of what I'd been in the midst of doing, all I could think about was his kiss. God, would he please kiss me again?

"I could command you to tell me the truth," he said, his voice so compelling and his eyes pulling me in, inviting me to drown in the darkness of his soul.

I wanted him. I wanted nothing *but* him. I'd tell him anything he asked, as long as I could have him. Yet, even as I opened my mouth to spill out my innermost thoughts, he stepped back.

"But I won't," he said, sounding distant again.

The urge to tell my secrets faded. I swallowed, shocked how close I'd come. What the hell had happened to me? How could I be so willing to give up Jeremy's future for a quick lay?

I blinked, trying to find my voice. "Do you want me to finish cleaning in here?" I asked, pocketing the pen that I never did find a place for. The other cameras would have to work. I prayed to whatever gods might still be listening to me that he wouldn't find them and catch on to my plans. I'd be dead. No lie.

"Your services are not needed in here," he said, clearly dismissing me with his tone.

With jangling nerves I feared he could hear, I

walked to the door, and as I stepped out into the hall, his voice stopped me.

"How are you feeling?"

It wasn't the question I was expecting. I turned to face him. "Better than I deserve," I said honestly.

He approached, his face unreadable and didn't stop until he came within inches of me. "You deserve so much more than you realize," he said softly, his eyes piercing my very soul as he brushed a lock of hair from my face. "Certainly, more than you've been given."

I sucked in a breath, not trusting myself to speak. He didn't know me. Didn't know what I'd done. What I'd lived through. What I was in the process of doing to him.

Truthfully, I was too jaded to judge who deserved what. But then, how could anyone know the weight of a person's soul? Mine or anyone else's?

"What darkness shadows your heart?" he asked, and I couldn't tell if it was rhetorical or not, but either way I didn't know how to answer.

"I could ask the same of you," I said, my voice catching on raw emotion.

"I've already shared with you my demons," he said, his lips inches from mine.

"I don't think those are all the demons you

harbor," I responded, desperate for the distance between us to disappear, but too scared to make it happen.

He inched closer, until our breath mingled. "It would take a lifetime to confess all my demons," he whispered, and I felt the kindred nature of his soul.

I couldn't fathom his demons, but I knew my own were terrifying enough, and I knew I was looking into the eyes of someone who had seen worse. Someone who had even done worse.

That should have terrified me, but instead it gave me comfort. Here was a man who would not be scared by the depths of my own darkness.

And I was about to betray him.

Shit.

I stepped back, catching my breath. "I, uh, should finish up the rest of the house before it gets too late."

I left quickly, feeling his eyes burning holes through me as I did.

That night the Count escorted another woman into his bedroom, and raw, unfettered jealousy poisoned me every minute she was with him. But in a plot twist I didn't see coming, she left shortly after she arrived, looking more than a little disappointed. She obviously didn't see that coming either, and by her scowl, I'd say she also didn't come. Poor girl. Really, I felt so bad for her.

When the Count came down to the kitchen just as I'd finished my shift, I paused and eyed him. "Rough night?" I asked.

He studied me a moment before replying, "My appetites seem to be changing."

My body buzzed with energy at that. Could it be our kiss distracted him as much as it had me? Dared I hope I played through his mind as much as he did mine?

But to what end?

So I could betray him in just a few days?

Still, I couldn't pull away from his gaze as he stood and walked over to me, stopping just shy of full body contact. He cupped my face and tilted his head. "Tell me, Kassandra, do you think about that kiss?"

I blinked, then nodded once, briefly. No point even trying to lie, not about that. The truth was written all over my face. I tried to contain my emotions and hold myself together, but already, my legs were turning to Jell-O, so my fortitude wouldn't last long.

The Count lowered his head and covered my mouth with his as one hand cupped my head and the other tugged at my hips to pull me close against him.

With a moan, I parted my lips, allowing his tongue to sweep inside and dance circles with mine. He tasted of fire, of mystery and power. I shivered as he devoured me with a dark mastery that sang to some deep part of me, and when his teeth grazed my lower lip, I arched against him. I needed more this time, so much more.

His fingers trailed down my cheek, over my neck, and further still, creating a path of burning need until he reached my breast. I gasped into his mouth as his thumb grazed my nipple through my shirt. *Yes. More.* I leaned into him, my body thirsting so desperately to feel a release with his.

Too soon, he pulled away, leaving my lips cold and my body melting.

With a resigned expression, he turned. "I will spend the evening in my quarters. Get some rest."

My mouth dropped open as he vanished through the kitchen door.

What. The. Hell?

Oh, this man was so damn infuriating. Teasing me, bringing me to the edge of everything and then just leaving me there alone? Just what kind of twisted game *was* this?

No, damnit. He'd satisfied an entire parade of women before me. Why leave *me* hanging? What did they have that I didn't? Well, probably a lot, but I refused to go there right now. Regardless of who had what, he couldn't treat me like this.

I didn't realize I'd followed him up the stairs until I stood at the very top and saw him at the end of the darkened hall, his hand on the knob of his bedroom door.

I didn't say anything. God, I wanted to. I wanted to shout at him, demand an explanation, demand that he finish what he'd started, but before I could even begin to organize the thoughts jumbling in my head, he stood before me.

Like he was just there, mere inches away. He'd just been at the edge of the hallway literally a blink ago. How? Sure, it was dark, but—

"Why are you here?" he queried, his eyes glittering despite the dim lighting.

"You can't just... you can't just leave me like that," I blurted.

A glint of amusement lit his eyes. "Pray tell, what should I have done?"

Take me on the kitchen table would have been nice. Or against the refrigerator. Or—

He stepped toward me then and backed me against the wall.

My breath hitched.

"Perhaps..." he rumbled, dragging the word out so long I could feel his chest vibrate. "Perhaps, I should have touched you more?"

Hell, yes. It was cruel to leave a girl on the edge like that. Especially with the gifts he obviously possessed. Yet still, under the spell of his gaze, I found myself rendered mute.

It didn't matter. His hands slid over me once again, outlining the contour of my hips as I lifted my mouth to meet his.

His kiss was different this time. Wilder. Darker. A kiss that shared not only pleasure but volumes of unspoken pain. I felt his neediness, his desire to belong, his wants, his despair, his loneliness. I'd seen glimpses of the darkness in him before, but this time, his kiss left no doubt. In him lived a void that matched mine.

I kissed him back, letting his lips pull from me, for the first time in my life, my own brand of pleasured pain. My naked true self.

Heat sparked, heralding the pleasure to come, but this time, we'd connected on a different level. This time, I needed more than his kiss. His lips tormented me. I had to have him inside me.

As if he'd read my thoughts, his hand skimmed over my hip and up. Magically, my jeans unbuttoned

—or had I done that myself?—and then, who cared how, his hands were under the waistband and hot against my flesh.

As his fingers slipped slowly down, he dropped his mouth against my neck to suck the tender flesh.

I shivered. I was so very wet. So ready. Wanting him to forgo the teasing and really touch me, I pushed up against him. Again, he read my thoughts, but then, with the way my body writhed in need, it wasn't a particularly hard thought to read. Still, I got what I wanted. At last. His fingers teased me, circling, pinching me into a frenzy until finally, Oh Blessed Heaven, he drove them inside me at last.

I climaxed at once, and as the intense storm of waves rippled through me, I collapsed against him. And just when I thought it was over, he nipped my neck and pushed his fingers deeper inside me and I came again.

I could hardly stand as waves of pleasures crashed into me. It felt as if every bone in my body had turned to liquid.

I looked up to see him watching me intensely.

"Like an instrument," he whispered, his fingers still teasing me.

I swallowed. If he kept playing with me like that,

I'd come again. I wasn't sure I could so quickly, without kicking off a migraine, anyway.

As before, he seemed unusually attuned to my inner thoughts, and with a last teasing movement of his fingers, he pulled out, but left me feeling branded by his touch, nonetheless.

He shifted. I could feel his hardness pressed against me, but when I reached for him, he drew back.

The next instant, he was gone, and at the same moment, his bedroom door clicked shut.

What the—

How could anyone move so fast? But then, maybe it was all a trick of the darkness. I braced myself against the wall, breathing heavily and unable to believe I'd just let the Count finger me.

What was I doing? He was my boss, not some guy I met at a bar and could forget about later. We'd definitely blurred the lines. And I still didn't even know his actual name. I winced. I'd thought looking him in the eye after a kiss was bad. Tomorrow would be much worse.

I returned to my room, a little puzzled as to why he hadn't let me touch him. He'd wanted me. I'd felt the evidence, hard and real. With someone else, I might have even felt a little rejected at the speed with which he'd run off, but he was different.

I didn't feel stung by the rejection so much as perplexed by his resistance to what was growing between us. Was it my status as his employee that kept him at arm's length… most of the time at least? Or was there something else going on?

My body buzzed with the energy of our encounter, but I didn't feel satisfied from it. Not the way I expected. I'd thought this would offer me relief, but now, I wanted the real thing. Small wonder the parade of women had rolled with him in bed all night.

Just what would that feel like?

I padded to my mirror and stared at my reflection as I ran my fingers over the trail he'd created with his mouth.

I saw it then. A small mark. A hickey? I peered closer. It wasn't the classical hickey, but just two little marks, tiny ones that barely broke the skin and positioned far apart, like a snake bite.

Or vampire. Ha!

Wanting to relieve every moment of the encounter, I dropped onto my bed, praying I'd dream of him all night.

· · ·

I DID DREAM ALL NIGHT, BUT NOT OF THE Count. This time, I had nightmares of Don and teddy bear cams that followed me around with glowing eyes recording and judging my every crime. I woke up with a sour taste in my mouth, as if even in my dreams I'd wanted to vomit.

I swung my legs out of bed, feeling like shit for so many reasons. Just who was I? The kind of girl who could make out with the Count and then set the stage so Don could rob him blind? Didn't that make me the whore my father accused me of being?

I stood in the shower for a long time, wanting the hot water to wash my problems down the drain, but wrinkled, pruned skin was the only thing it deigned to give me.

After dressing, I decided to check on Jeremy, so I got my phone out of the drawer and headed to what was becoming my favorite spot in the garden outside. I idly wondered what would happen if I used my phone in the house. How would the Count know? I had a gut feeling he would. Somehow, he would.

When my phone finally turned on, I saw three missed calls flashing and voicemails from Jeremy's school.

My heart jumped into my throat and my knees shook as I hit the callback button. They never called unless there was a problem. And I had enough of those already.

"Mr. Prichard's office."

"I'm calling about Jeremy. This is Kassandra, his sister."

"Oh, right." There was a pause. "He's with the school nurse—"

"Nurse? What happened?" I interrupted.

Already, I was pulling my keys out of my pocket and heading to my car.

I hardly heard her reply, "There was a...conflict, an...incident. He..."

The tiny voice jabbered on, but I didn't need to hear more.

I knew what 'incident' meant. It was code for 'beaten by bullies.'

They'd beaten Jeremy.

Again.

wollen eye. Bloodied nose. Maybe even a hairline-cracked rib. Urgent care discharged us with prescription-strength Advil and instructions to rest. I helped Jeremy into the car, not because he couldn't walk. He could, slowly. But because it felt like I was protecting him, even though I was obviously way too late on the protection front. Still, he needed mothering, and though I was a poor substitute, I had to do what I could.

"I tried ignoring them," he said again as I slid into the driver's seat.

"Yeah, sometimes ignoring doesn't work," I offered grimly. Ignoring Don hadn't produced any magical results for me. How could I have thought it would for Jeremy?

I blinked back tears and turned the keys. I couldn't just abandon Jeremy at the hotel. And I certainly couldn't take him home, not in this condition. At home, he had to be swift and nimble on his feet.

Plus, the ER doc had made it clear he needed to be supervised in case of concussion. So, no school for a few days.

I pulled out of the parking lot, onto the road, and drove as I weighed my options. Well…truthfully, there was only one option, and it weighed a shit-ton.

I had to keep Jeremy safe.

And I had to work.

"Where are we going?" Jeremy asked.

The Count had said to keep my personal life out of his business. And showing up with my bloodied brother in tow was nothing if not personal.

Yet, did I have a choice?

I didn't answer Jeremy and kept on driving. When I finally pulled into the private driveway and drove up the long, winding road, he asked again, "Where are we going?"

"We're here," I said as the mansion came into view.

Jeremy stared, wide-eyed. "Is this where you've been living?"

My stomach dropped when I realized what this must look like to him. I was living the rich life while he'd hidden out in shitty motels. What a wretch of a sister he must have thought me.

I parked the car and then answered, "Yes. I'm the housekeeper here and it's a live-in situation. I don't think you can stay without me losing my job, but you can come inside until I figure out something."

"Okay."

His small voice broke my heart. My knuckles turned white as I clutched the steering wheel. I was so tired of my heart breaking all of the time. With a deep breath, I got out of the car and helped him out.

He followed me inside, limping in pain and trying to hide it. I did my best not to hover over him, but it was hard. I wanted to give him a better life, but I wasn't succeeding.

Depressed and on edge, I led him up to my room. It took awhile to get there, and I felt bad about making him navigate up the stairs, but I only felt comfortable having him rest on my bed. I couldn't impose on the Count anymore than I already had by installing Jeremy in one of the guest rooms without permission…even though he'd probably never notice… but still.

"Nice room," Jeremy said as he hobbled to the bed.

"Take a nap," I ordered as I dropped his Advil on the side table. "I'll wake you up in a few." As soon as I figured out what to do with him.

He was out before I even reached the door.

THIS TIME, I LET MYSELF INTO THE COUNT'S office as the very first order of business. I couldn't risk cutting it so close to evening anymore. And while I was ninety-nine percent sure he wasn't awake, my heart still pounded as I quickly downloaded the files from each camera onto a USB thumb drive and reset them.

I'd originally planned on driving to Jeremy's hotel to use his school laptop to play back the camera results, but with his school bag conveniently in my car, I didn't have far to go this time.

I settled in the back seat, dug through his backpack, and turned the machine on. Ten minutes later, I was flipping the lid shut in disappointment. The Count hadn't even entered his office, let alone opened the safe.

Oh, well. I still had five days, didn't I? I'd succeed. I *would*.

And right now, I couldn't waste time worrying about the future, not when I had Jeremy hiding out upstairs.

My shift wasn't for a few more hours, so I went to the kitchen and made some pasta and garlic bread, Jeremy's favorites. At least he'd wake up to a good meal, for once. I brought it all upstairs on a tray that I left by his bed, then I ate my portion in silence in front of the fireplace as I obsessed over what, if anything, I should tell the Count.

Maybe, I could hide Jeremy for one night and sneak him out in the morning? Surely, the Count wouldn't even know he'd been here. This place was so big, and Jeremy looked so pale, with deep purple bruises under his eyes. He needed rest. He needed to feel safe.

And the school was getting suspicious. His teacher said he's been falling asleep in class and seemed more anxious than usual. They wanted to talk to our father, but I put them off. For now.

After I finished eating, I checked on Jeremy one last time, drawing the covers up to his chin and tucking him in more snugly. He smiled in his sleep and nestled down in the pillows, no doubt, on some deep level remembering mom, so I hummed a song she used to sing to him when he was a baby.

Sleeping, he looked even younger than normal, so innocent and fragile.

And that settled things for me. I made up my mind right there, even knowing I'd just invited the universe to bite me in the ass, as it so often enjoyed doing.

It didn't matter.

I'd take the hits for this kid any day.

I kissed his forehead, then closed the door softly behind me as I went downstairs to start my shift.

When I saw the Count, I'd have my say, and he would listen. I wouldn't lie or break his rules, at least not in this. But I wouldn't back down, either. I was doing all this for Jeremy, and right now what my brother needed most was me and a safe place to live until I could get us out of here. So, I was going to give him that.

I WAS MOPPING THE KITCHEN FLOOR WHEN I FELT the Count's presence before he spoke.

"Who is the bleeding child in your room?"

I looked up, propping my fist on my hip and holding the mop in my other hand.

The thought that he'd visited my room pleased the dark, aroused side of me even as the rest of me got pissed—and a little scared. I couldn't lose this job. Not now. I had a whole thing planned in my head, not expecting he'd beat me to the punch and ruin my lead in.

"Well?" he didn't wait to prompt.

"My brother." I jammed the mop back into the bucket so hard the water slopped on the floor. "He needs to stay here awhile. And before you toss me out, just think for a second, will you? How can I send him home to my father? You've seen what he's like. Jeremy's weak enough as it is, don't you think?"

The Count looked at me from under furrowed brows. Damn it. What a poker face. You'd think after our recent intimacy that I'd understand him even an inkling more, but I saw nothing in that face.

Then, he whirled and just left me there.

I dropped the mop and ran to my room. Arriving out of breath, I twisted the doorknob, only to hear the Count's voice already from inside.

I shoved the door open so hard it bounced off the wall.

The Count sat on the edge of the bed, supporting Jeremy as he drank from a goblet. They both looked at me, surprised.

I just stared, mouth agape. How the hell had the Count gotten here so fast? He must have prepped the drink before he'd even asked me about Jeremy, but then…why had he even bothered to ask?

Jeremy grinned and waved for me to join them. "The Count is giving me his family recipe. Says it'll help and it's all natural."

If it was the same mixture that he'd given to me, then I knew Jeremy would be healing fast. I walked to the bed and sat on the opposite side of the Count and brushed a lock of Jeremy's hair out of his eyes. He needed a haircut.

When my brother finished the goblet, the Count gently eased him back on the pillow. "You'll sleep deeply and wake up feeling refreshed, Jeremy," he assured.

With the way Jeremy's eyes drooped, I doubt he even heard. I knew he'd be asleep in minutes.

As the Count took his goblet and walked out of the room silently, I followed at his heels.

Out in the hall, I grabbed his arm. "Thank you," I said, nodding my head at the bedroom door. "He hasn't seen a lot of kindness in his life."

"He is a special boy," the Count murmured, and when he looked down at me, I saw the empathy behind his expression. Then, he added, "But he cannot stay here."

Even though I knew I didn't have the right to

complain—rules and all—I opened my mouth to protest.

The Count raised a hand to silence me. "My life... this house... isn't suited for children."

I snorted at that. "You think my house is? At least here, he won't get beaten up. He'll have food. He'll have love." I swallowed the lump in my throat. "He'll have me."

The Count said nothing. He just towered over me, his face a mask once more.

I didn't let that stop me. "The thing is, I can't live here if I can't keep Jeremy with me. I could still work for you. Do all the things you need me to. But I need to take care of my brother, and that means I need access to my phone at all times. He was stuck in the nurse's station for hours because they couldn't reach me. I can't do this to him. Not after everything he's been through."

By the end of my passionate speech, I was standing on the tip of my toes, hands clenched into fist. Yes, I risked everything by trying to change the rules, but did I have a choice? I could only hope the Count had a heart somewhere in that broad, chiseled chest—despite the fact I hadn't heard it beat.

"You would give up this job to be with him?" The Count raised a dark brow.

My heart sank at the question's direction, but in this, I had no problem telling the truth. "Yes."

"He's lucky to have you."

A tear escaped down my cheek.

The Count frowned and wiped the pad of his thumb across my skin to catch it. "Then you wish to renegotiate the terms of your employment?"

That didn't sound like a fully closed door. "Yeah. I guess I do," I said.

"And what do you propose?"

My mind raced to come up with an answer I could live with. "Let us both stay here, with full access to our phones and computers. We can share my room if you don't want to give up a guest room." I could live with that. Easy. But as for his side of the deal, I had only one card. "You can dock my pay to compensate."

I could tell he wasn't impressed. "Money is a triviality to me," he said.

When he didn't continue, my heart began to pound. I didn't have anything else to bargain. Shit.

"However." His gaze shifted to something behind me, and the way he stared made me want to turn around to see what he was staring at. "I will require other services from you in exchange."

My back stiffened. Was he putting me on that

level, then? "What kind of services," I grated, teeth clenched.

His eyes immediately returned to mine. "Not what you're thinking." He stepped closer to me then, bringing his body an inch away from mine. "I was under the impression this part of our relationship was mutual?"

My breathing shallowed as his scent overwhelmed me. "It was," I whispered. "Is." How could he—without even touching me—make me so weak with need? I licked my dry lips and asked again, "So, what services?"

Again, his gaze turned unseeing as he focused over my shoulder. "Those will become apparent as the need arises," he replied, not answering the question at all.

I was about to insist he ask nothing illegal, but who the hell was I kidding? I was way past worrying about what was legal and what wasn't. And anyway, for Jeremy, I'd do it all.

"So, we have a deal?" I asked, lifting my hand for a handshake, but there was so very little room between us, my hand grazed his hip.

He caught my fingers in his and running the pad of his thumb over my palm, elegantly brought my hand to his lips. God, the gesture was so practiced, so smooth. And his lips, kissing me so gently, felt like a butterfly landing on my skin. Doubtless, he must have kissed countless women this way, but still, I felt special. Unique. My knees trembled.

"We have a deal, Kassandra," his deep baritone rumbled beneath my skin. "Jeremy stays away from my private suite and office, and he follows the rules set forth. If either of you break them, you both are out. There will be no further negotiation. Are we clear?"

I nodded. "Crystal."

He let me go, trailing his thumb again in a way that increased the intimacy of the simple gesture of letting go of my hand. I watched him, my pulse racing, as he took the hall in long strides and vanished into the darkness.

Jeremy could stay.

If only this situation could last. If only I didn't have to screw up this whole thing in less than a week.

But the clock was ticking. And if Don got to Jeremy, no amount of magic family potion would cure him then. I didn't have a choice. I had to follow Don's instructions to the letter.

10

*W*hen I woke the next afternoon, it was to hear Jeremy whistling under his breath.

I'd fallen asleep on the couch. I propped myself on an elbow and looked up to see my brother resting on his stomach on a fully made bed, reading a book, face relaxed and whistling softly as he always did when he concentrated on something interesting. He'd obviously been up for a bit.

I'd really done it. I'd secured him a safe place to stay—with me even. And after…after Don did what he did, Jeremy and I would be off to Canada with our fake IDs, and no one would ever threaten us again.

"Feeling better?" I asked as I sat up.

Jeremy rolled himself off the bed, a gesture that should've been impossible with a broken rib.

"I'm awesome." He grinned, jumping to his feet.

The Count should sell that potion. He'd make millions. But then… I glanced around at the luxury of my room, and that was just a single room in a mansion of many. Well, maybe that was where his wealth came from?

I turned back to my brother. God, it was so nice to see him happy. "The Count said you can stay here, for a bit," I said. "But there are rules."

"Rules? Right."

I led Jeremy down to the kitchen, reciting the rules along the way. Then, I made him breakfast. A shake, like I made myself. Now that I knew he was going to be here for a bit, I'd have to hit the grocery store for things he liked to eat. He wasn't a picky eater, but he did prefer to stay in the realm of the familiar. Standard things like, eggs, white bread, Mac 'n Cheese, pasta.

"And school?" Jeremy asked when I turned off the blender. His expression had turned guarded.

Yeah, I wasn't shipping him back to those bullies anytime soon. "Urgent care said you'd be out of school for at least a week," I said. "And even though

I'm sure you could run a marathon right now, you're out for the week."

Wow. Two wide grins in a single day, and we'd just gotten started. I found myself grinning back, despite all the shit that was going on. My thoughts darkened for a moment. Don. The robbery. What the hell was I doing? But I brushed off the worry, at least for now. Seeing that grin on Jeremy's peaked face made it all worthwhile. I chose to bask in that for as long as I could.

As I rinsed out the blender and our glasses, my eyes caught on a piece of paper resting on the countertop.

Eggs. Gruyere Cheese. Rosemary.

The list went on, each item written in elegant calligraphy, complete with flourishes.

I blinked. So, a grocery list, Count style? I guess he was getting tired of eating whatever ethereal food he'd been downing besides his strange wine. Some-where, deep inside, part of me heaved a sigh of relief. It was an odd reaction. I guess I'd been bothered by his strange dining habits—or lack thereof.

"I've got to head out," I told Jeremy as I snagged the list. "You stay here and study. You've got a science project, right?"

He didn't mind staying in my room. I dumped off

his school backpack on the bed, and before I left, made him recite the rules and pinky-promise not to explore.

I'd just dropped the last grocery bag into the trunk of my car when hands gripped my shoulders from behind.

I whirled, lashing out, as I heard the word, "Four."

Don grabbed my wrist before my fist could connect with his face.

"Whoa, girl." His eyes took on that sick mix of anger and interest. Violence always turned him on. "Maybe you should detour over to my place, huh?"

"Only got four days, Don," I snapped, wrenching myself free. I hated his skin touching mine. "Gotta go."

He blocked my path. "So, you got Jeremy living with you now, huh?"

How the hell did he know that? Was he stalking me?

"Just don't get any ideas in that head of yours," he warned, flicking me on the side of the head. "Stick to the plan. Or else."

He walked away with that self-important swagger

of his and I dashed inside my car and locked the door, my palms slick with sweat and my heart hammering against my chest.

How did he know so much about mine and Jeremy's day-to-day life? And the Count's business, too?

It struck me as I pulled off the road and into the mansion's long driveway.

Don must have bugged the place. And he was listening to everything we did and said.

I CHECKED THE CAMERAS, BUT I DIDN'T SEE anything. My mind wasn't really on the safe's code, anyway. I was still trying to figure out how Don was spying on us. He'd either set up surveillance before I'd even arrived at the mansion for my interview, or else he'd dropped a few bugs the night I'd forgotten to lock the door. In either case, a thorough cleaning job was on the books tonight.

Since I couldn't afford any more gadgets, I'd done a little research on how to locate bugs on the cheap. Brute force and using your cellphone were my only two options. At least I'd gotten my phone back and wouldn't have to sneak it in for this.

I inspected the entryway first, thoroughly 'dusting' every lamp, unscrewing every lightbulb, and peeking under every piece of furniture. The suit of armor in the corner was particularly time-consuming.

My search turned up nothing, and before I moved on to the next room, I called the bank. Why the bank? Well, according to the internet, wireless cameras and microphones emitted specific radio frequencies that interfered with cellphone signals. Apparently, you just had to walk around on a call and if you heard clicks in a specific area...voila, bug found. And since I didn't have anyone I actually wanted to *talk* to that long, I'd settled for the number that always put me on hold.

I walked around the entryway slowly, listening to crappy elevator music and on the alert for clicking sounds.

"Bug free," I muttered when I'd completed the circle.

One room down.

At least fifty more to go.

I winced, grabbed my supplies, and kicked the rolling cannister vacuum into the next room.

I'd prioritized searching the rooms encompassing all routes from the front door to the kitchen where I'd found Don that night. By the time I'd retraced that path, my back ached, and I had every cheesy piano rendition on the bank's waiting loop memorized.

The delicious scent of rosemary greeted my nostrils when I stepped into the kitchen, but at the sight of Jeremy standing at the stove, a chef's hat perched sideways on his head and a wooden spoon in his hand, my heart jumped into my throat.

God. He'd made a mess. There had to be at least a dozen eggshells on the island mixed with broccoli stalks and the roots of green onions. It. Was. A. Fricking. Mess.

And he was grinning?

Yeah, the grin melted my anger, a little. I mean, I was glad to see Jeremy so blasted happy, but not at the risk of angering the Count. Rules were rules. And while the Count hadn't explicitly said 'No Jeremy cooking in the kitchen' I was pretty sure at least one of his rules covered Jeremy raiding the fridge and making a mess. Somehow.

"What is it?" Jeremy asked, reading my face and turning tense.

I glanced over my shoulder, nervously. "Maybe it's best not to use the stove, huh?" No point in testing just how kid-friendly the Count was. "If you're hungry, I'll make you something."

I eyed the remains of the Rosemary stalks mixed in all the eggshells. Then the alarm bells went off.

Shit.

Shit. Shit. Shit. Jeremy hadn't just raided the fridge. He'd used the Count's fancy ingredients. He'd even opened the package of Brie and left it in a pile of trash on the corner of the island. The store would be closed before I could get there to buy more.

"Jeremy, what have you done?" I choked. I hurried to the cheese, praying I could salvage some of it, despite the egg whites dripping into the package. Shit. Could you wash cheese?

Jeremy giggled.

I glanced back at him, astonished to see him grinning from ear-to-ear. "That smelled so bad, Kass. Goat cheese is soooo much better."

"You…can't do this, Jeremy," I hissed. "Take off the hat and hand me that spoon."

"Why?" Jeremy frowned.

Because I've already annoyed the hell out of my boss enough this week? Make that, month? And when he finds out—

"Yes, pray tell, why?"

It took a second to register that the deep voice coming from behind me belonged to the Count himself.

Shit. What could I possibly say? My brain went numb. I just stood there, trying my best to concoct an excuse when the Count walked into my field of vision.

What the—

He stood on the other side of the island with a bag of flour in his hand and a white apron tied low over his lean hips. He'd unbuttoned the top two buttons of his white shirt, and the way the fabric stretched over his broad shoulders made me want to unbutton the rest.

God, he really rocked that apron. Somehow, it just drew my gaze to his thighs, so defined, sculpted. I could imagine those muscles rippling beneath me so sensuously as I straddled him. I caught my breath and with difficulty, dragged my eyes back to his face.

He stood there, watching me with an arched, wicked brow, a brow that told me he'd followed the essence of my thoughts, at the very least, if not the details, as well.

"Would you care to join us?" he asked, peering down at me from under half-hooded eyes.

My insides melted. "I...uh..." Yeah, brilliant response there, Kass.

"The Count is teaching me how to 'whip up a soufflé'," Jeremy said from the stove.

Right. The stove. I turned toward my brother, mostly to escape the Count's carnal gaze. After all, I couldn't risk just what I might do if I held still under that spell for too long.

Then, the sight of Jeremy's happy face cleared all other thoughts out of my mind. Wow. I hadn't seen my brother so happy since...well, I can't recall when.

"A souffle?" I repeated belatedly.

"The Brie cheese was... well, it smelled rotten," Jeremy continued, waving his wooden spoon at the pot bubbling on the stove. "So, we're changing the recipe."

"Indeed," the Count agreed.

He brushed his hand low over the base of my spine as he passed. I shivered. And I know he saw, because I could see his cheek move into a smile, even at the angle from which I stood.

I didn't move. How could I? The sight of Jeremy and the Count discussing the recipe tugged at my heart and made me feel all warm inside.

"Cream of Tartar," Jeremy tapped the wooden spoon on a "Food and Wine" Magazine propped up against an empty eggshell carton.

"Must be in the pantry." The Count nodded, and then he was heading back my way.

I dropped my gaze.

He slowed behind me, long enough to trail his

fingers down my spine before he paused to breathe in my ear, "Like an instrument."

God, I wanted him.

Then, he moved away.

It was just as well. With Jeremy in the room, there'd be no strapping the Count down to the island and having my way. I blew a heated breath. *Time to behave, Kass.*

"You can help, too," Jeremy offered.

"I can't," I told my brother. "I've got to work." I had bugs to find. Then, I eyed the messy kitchen and added, "And don't forget to clean up your mess."

He laughed.

I skipped out before the Count could emerge from the pantry once again to play me like whatever instrument he was imagining.

"We'll call you when they're done," Jeremy called after me.

I smiled and dove back into my work.

Several times, I passed outside the kitchen door to hear Jeremy and the Count talking about various things as they puttered about, clanging pots and pans. The topics ranged from the Lunar effect, to aerodynamics, and on to Falconry. Falconry? I eavesdropped a bit on that one and learned that once, long ago, the

Count liked to ride horses and hunt with his favorite Peregrine, Ecaterina.

When the souffles were ready, I was summoned back to the kitchen by a phone call. I was happy for the break. My knees ached from crawling around the floor, looking under all the furniture.

"Perfection," the Count was saying as I entered.

They'd cleaned the kitchen, lit a few candles, and placed the souffles on a plate in the center of the island. They looked like something out of a magazine.

"Do they taste as good as they look?" I asked Jeremy.

He shrugged an 'I dunno' and said, "Dive in."

There were only two plates. "I'm working—" I began.

"Nonsense," the Count interrupted, sending me a look. "I'm not a slave owner. And I did invite you to enjoy a meal with your brother."

The souffles smelled tempting and they looked so fancy. "But yourself?" I asked, puzzled.

"He says he'll eat later," Jeremy chimed in as he cozied up to the island. "Don't know about you two, but I'm sure eating now."

I watched the Count cross to the fridge and take out one of his dark wine bottles. Strange. I'd yet to see him eat, but then, maybe he had a health condition. Maybe.

I eyed his muscular form as he poured the last of the red wine into his goblet. Nah, he was the picture of health. And he was strong. He'd dangled my dad as if he'd weighed a feather, and he'd carried me around without even needing an extra breath. No doubt, he had one of those pure, strict diets, the kind that didn't allow things like eggs, butter, and cheese. But somehow allowed wine?

The candlelight played over his handsome face as he just leaned against the counter, taking the occasional sip of his drink as Jeremy and I downed several souffles each.

The conversation was a wild one with Jeremy involved, and we spent the better part of an hour laughing—the Count included until finally, he took his leave.

"Shit," I glanced at my watch. I had so much work to do.

I left Jeremy to put the food away and zipped back up the stairs to doggedly search for Don's bugs.

If only I had a way out.

If only I didn't have to help Don and betray the Count. I'd never met anyone like him. Abrupt and commanding, yet kind and surprisingly tender. Sexy. God, yes, sexy. And mysteriously dark…

Shit.

I was falling, totally falling for my boss/target.

That wouldn't end well at all.

11

The next few days flew past. I inspected every inch of the house, and I'd listened to the bank's music so much I caught myself singing the sappy songs in the shower. Still, after all that effort, I hadn't found a thing, I didn't have time to order any of those fancy devices.

It was late when I made it back to my room. Jeremy had fallen asleep on the couch while reading a book. I had just enough energy to toss a blanket over him before collapsing into bed, exhausted.

My cellphone vibrated just as sleep was settling over me. I moaned and glanced at the screen.

"I"

. . .

ONE? THEN, REALIZATION FLOODED. SHIT. ONE day left. Twenty-four hours.

I'd run out of time.

I sat up, suddenly wide-awake.

No way was sleep coming for me now. Instead, I was visited by the ghosts of bad life choices. The first ghost berated me for betraying the Count. The second one showed me what would happen should I fail, and Don dug his claws of revenge into his pound of flesh owed, only it wasn't my flesh he would collect on.

No matter what happened, I was going to be miserable, but wasn't that just par for the course of my life?

Thanks, universe. Thanks for all the help.

Sick of tossing and turning, I slipped out of bed and padded quietly into the kitchen. After retrieving a tub of raw cookie dough from the fridge, I sat at the island and ate my feelings.

Part of me wondered what would happen should I approach the Count and tell him everything. I nearly did, yet deep inside, I just couldn't take the chance. Yeah, he'd been spending a lot of time with Jeremy, and I'd let myself fall deeper into the spell of attraction, but that didn't mean I could trust him. The closer I got to him, the more my instincts screamed that he was a man of many secrets. Many. And in my experience, those kinds of secrets weren't the good kind. Long story short, I finally came to the conclusion I just couldn't risk Jeremy's life and future on such an unknown.

And that meant I had to go through with Don's plan.

My heart tore, but I had to choose. It was Jeremy or the Count. It wasn't much of a battle. Jeremy would always win.

And with that, I had only one path before me. I had to help Don. I had to freaking force the Count into his office.

I tapped my fingers on the cookie dough container like a drum. How could I get the Count to open his safe?

I tried to come up with a plan, but my mind either wanted to wallow in self-pity over betraying the Count or it wanted me to forget everything and go hunt down some Tums.

Finally, a good six Tums later, I had my plan.

It wasn't the best, but it was the best I could do.

. . .

"I need money."

The Count arched an elegant brow and waited where he stood in his private library, book in hand.

Hell, he wasn't making this easy. Did he enjoy watching people squirm? As dark and brooding as he was, he didn't seem like the type to lord it over others. In fact, he'd seemed quite opposite.

I swallowed. I couldn't fail. This had to work. I didn't have a backup plan. "It's Jeremy."

"Jeremy?"

"He's talented. Brilliant, actually. You've seen that. He needs supplies for the science fair. I didn't save back any money this time."

He just waited, damn him. And why did he have to look so smoking hot, his muscles outlined so temptingly in the dim lighting?

I took a fortifying breath. So, he wanted the truth, did he? Well, in this, I could give him the truth. Lots of it. "Truth is, I got myself into a mountain of trouble and debt. Pure stupidity on my part. But I'm paying it back, and the guy's an asshole. I used pretty much my last entire paycheck on the first payment and the rest on Jeremy. I've got nothing left, and I wouldn't ask, only Jeremy's science fair hit me out of the blue. I don't need much, just a little."

I guess he heard the authenticity in my voice,

because he strode out of his library and in the hallway, lifted his hand. "Follow," he said.

I did, heart pounding.

He led me to his office, unlocked the door, and
disappeared inside.

I almost called him back. Almost. I'm ashamed to
say how close it was. I felt like the worst kind of jerk.
Jeremy should always be first. How could it even be a
contest?

"Come in, Kassandra," the Count called me from
inside.

Showtime.

I entered his office to find he'd lit a candle on the
edge of his desk. He stood before the large oil
painting of the dragon and the beautiful sword-
wielding woman.

Please, please let the cameras be angled right.
Please.

The painting slid aside, revealing the safe.

I could scarcely watch. This was my one and only
shot. I'd run out of luck and out of time.

Then, his fingers danced over the keypad as he
plugged in the security code and all I could do was
pray. Does that sound bad? I'd been a good person…
well, lately. And did the fact I prayed for success so I

could steal cancel the whole praying thing out? Making it all null and void?

I wasn't raised religious, so I wasn't sure how all that worked.

I heard the safe swing open.

I didn't look. I couldn't. Bile rose in my throat and I swallowed it down with a grimace. Only when I heard the Count move to his desk did I finally raise my eyes.

He stood there, counting his hundred-dollar bills. "Here. Five hundred should be enough?" He raised a quizzical brow.

What the hell kind of science fair had he ever participated in that needed five hundred dollars?

"Plenty," I whispered hoarsely. "Thanks."

God, I felt like the worst kind of human.

"My pleasure, Kassandra."

Now, I felt even worse.

I left, clutching the money tightly in my fingers and feeling them burn in my own version of Hell.

THE NEXT DAY, I FORCED MYSELF TO WAIT UNTIL noon to collect the cameras. I'd never seen the Count out of his bedroom at that time, and as this was my last day, I couldn't afford to take any kind of chance.

It was Saturday, and since Jeremy wasn't in school, he sat in the kitchen, writing the pros and cons of each Science Fair project idea. He'd narrowed his choices down to three.

"Be right back," I murmured as I slipped his laptop out of his backpack and ran to the nearest guest room.

My fingers trembled as I downloaded the file from first camera onto the USB drive. "Please," I whispered a prayer. "Pleeeease let me see the code."

Carefully, I inserted the USB drive into the computer and began playing the file. Since I'd been in the room, I knew the time already, so I skipped through the hours of dark, empty office until a ray of light fell across the screen.

I tensed.

That must have been when the Count had opened the door.

A flame danced against the wall when the candle was lit.

I held my breath. I saw myself standing at the edge of the screen. *Yes.* This was it. And there was the Count, moving toward the—

What the hell?

I hit the pause button and stared at the computer screen. What the hell was I looking at? Clothes?

Just…clothes? I could see the Count's shirt and pants…but no head…or hands.

Was the camera defective?

I hit the play button. The clothes walked to the painting and the painting slid aside. I fast-forwarded through the footage. No head. No hands. Just his clothes, moving around the room, along with the floating stack of money.

"Has to be the camera," I muttered under my breath as I reached for the next camera, the Velcro one, and downloaded the file. Nervously, I clicked the play button.

"Nothing. Nothing. Nothing," I mumbled as I sped through the file showing the empty office. "There, the light."

The candle was lit and the Count approached the safe, this time from a different angle.

And…this time…shit. It was the same. I saw myself enter. I had a head. And hands. As expected. But…the Count? *Where the hell were his body parts?*

I rewound and played the file again, probably a dozen times or more, trying to understand.

It wasn't until the last time I ran through the footage that I saw the safe keypad and the little lights flickering around each number as the Count's invisible fingers depressed the keys.

The code. I'd captured the code.

In a daze, I returned Jeremy's laptop. I think he asked me something, but I really don't recall. I just stood there, leaning against the kitchen island as I massaged the back of my neck.

"Good afternoon," a voice spoke behind me.

I screeched and whirled, only to see Leonard entering the kitchen, suitcase in hand.

"Forgive me, Miss Kassandra," he said with a warm smile on his gaunt face. "I didn't mean to frighten you."

I swallowed. "You're back."

"I am," Leonard acknowledged.

He vanished through the door and returned with a large antique chest, banded with iron and securely fastened with a padlock. After setting it down next to his suitcase, he straightened and dusted his hands.

"Did you enjoy your vacation?" I asked. He looked even thinner than when he'd left—and he'd been rail thin to begin with. Didn't people usually gain weight on holidays?

Leonard's eyes flicked to the chest and then back to me. "A success. Thank you."

Success. I batted down a budding interest in the chest's contents. Really, I wouldn't want to know. What if it was something weird? Like a pair of walking clothes?

"And I'm glad to be back," Leonard continued, and then turned toward Jeremy. "And this, I presume, is your brother?"

I nodded. It was odd, wasn't it, just how much these people seemed to know. First Don, and now Leonard...but then, to be fair, who else would the boy in the kitchen be besides my brother? And I'd probably told Leonard about him... hadn't I? Or likely the Count had communicated with Leonard in his absence. That made the most sense.

"I'm Jeremy," Jeremy introduced himself, apparently growing impatient for me to do the honors.

"Pleased to meet you," Leonard bowed. "Call me Leonard, if you please."

As they exchanged pleasantries, my mind wandered back to the odd video footage. No. Freaking. Clothes. There had to be an explanation. I grabbed my phone, searched on the internet for camera malfunctions, and began scanning the various articles.

"Miss Kassandra?"

I blinked and looked up. Jeremy had vanished

from the kitchen. Leonard hadn't. He stood next to his chest; his eyes locked onto me in open curiosity.

"Miss Kassandra?" he repeated.

I realized then that I must look a little odd, clutching my phone and ignoring everyone as I frantically flipped through search results.

"Has something happened?" Leonard pressed.

Like a video of just the Count's clothes walking around in his office? Without the Count inside them? Of course, I could never show him that.

"No." I shook my head. I had to play things cool, safe. And anyway, maybe Leonard didn't show up on cameras, either. He did look strange, so tall and thin. "It's been fine here, but glad to have you back."

He nodded and didn't say anything.

Feeling the need to fill the silence, I said, "The Count is letting Jeremy stay here for a bit, and he's changed the rules. He allowed me my phone." I held up my phone as if that proved I wasn't breaking the rules. I rolled my eyes at myself and kept babbling, "It's been interesting while you were out. Learned a few things. You know, about souffles and falconry."

"Falconry?" Leonard's head tilted to the side with interest.

"You're not a Falcon-ist?" What were they called?

"Falconer?" he politely supplied the word. "Good

lord, no. That sport went out of fashion a good two hundred years ago, maybe longer."

Well, the Count hadn't gotten the notice. The fondness in his voice couldn't be missed when he'd spoken of Ecaterina.

"Falconry," Leonard murmured as he returned to the chest.

I drew a steadying breath and dove back into my own business. Why was I psyching myself out? There had to be a rational explanation for the video glitches, right? Like the camera glitching out on skin color. I felt good for about two seconds before I recalled it hadn't erased *me* at all. But then, maybe just that section of the camera hadn't been functioning...on both cameras. Well...it *could* happen. Couldn't it?

Or maybe it was some kind of a laser shield over the safe that interfered with video recordings. That was a thing, wasn't it?

"Are you certain nothing has happened, Miss Kassandra?" Leonard stood by the chest just watching me, brows furrowed in a perplexed line.

"I'm fine. Really," I insisted, plastering a big, fake smile on my face.

My phone chose that moment to ping, announcing the arrival of a message. I didn't have to look. I already knew who it was. But I looked anyway.

"THIRTY MINUTES."

I DREW A SHARP BREATH. TECHNICALLY, I HAD longer than thirty minutes left. I had about four hours, but it didn't really matter. I had the code. I'd give the damn thing to Don, hightail it back, pick up Jeremy and go.

The phone pinged again.

"OR ELSE..."

RIGHT. AGAIN, ANOTHER PING.

"MEET ME HERE."

A LOCATION POPPED UP ON THE SCREEN.
Now, there was no way out.

I pulled up behind the grocery store and parked my car next to a group of green, overflowing garbage dumpsters. Flies buzzed around the rotten fruit and veggies that had fallen onto the pavement. A health hazard if I'd ever seen one.

And trust Don to pick such a disgusting location...but then, it matched.

I clutched the key to the Count's office in my hand so hard the metal grooves made angry red marks in my skin. The small slip of paper with the code to the safe burned a hole in the pocket of my jeans. I pulled it out and looked at the numbers again, though I had them memorized twice over.

I checked the location on my phone.

I had the right place, but where was—

Don's black Dodge Ram with tinted windows tore around the corner of the building, swerving a little as he headed straight toward me. He waited until I lost my nerve and dove for the passenger seat before squealing to a stop, less than two feet away.

"Chicken shit," he snorted as he hopped out of his truck. "You're nothing but a chicken shit. It's a miracle you pulled this off."

Ten minutes, Kass. In ten minutes, this will all be over. You've got that five hundred dollars hidden in the trunk. It's enough to cover the gas to get you and Jeremy to Canada. All you have to do is pick him up from school and just drive. Forget the IDs, forget the—

The passenger door yanked open and Don thrust his hand inside. "The code? The key?"

I swallowed and forced myself not to think as I slapped them both into his sweaty palm.

He studied my offerings as if they might take flight. "These better be real," he said. "I know how to get to you and the boy if they're not."

I nodded. "They are."

Don't think. Don't think how you've just betrayed the Count. *Damn it. Don't think.*

"Slide over," Don barked.

Shit. I didn't want him in my car, but I had no

way of stopping him. He already had the door open. I scooted back to the driver's seat. "You've got what you wanted," I said. "Deal's done."

Don chuckled as he crammed his long legs into my car and closed the door. "Key," he said, holding up the key in one hand and then, the paper in the other. "Code."

"Yeah."

"Good, now use them."

"What?

"You didn't think that *I* was going to break in when you're already there?" He looked at me with an incredulous expression. "Open that damn safe and bring me the contents."

He slammed both the key and the code onto the dashboard with such force that I cringed. Yeah, I got the message. He was letting me know I'd be the dashboard if I refused.

"That wasn't the deal," I croaked, my throat drying up like a parched desert. Despair churned deep inside me. I should have known. I should have freaking known. This wasn't going to end. He was never going to hold his end of the bargain. He'd be blackmailing me forever. Why, oh why, had I ever trusted him? Why the hell do criminals trust other criminals?

"I'm in charge here, Kass," he ranted. "And what I say the deal is, the deal is. That's the way it—"

"There's something new," I interrupted as a half-baked—ok, quarter-baked at best—plan began to form. He wanted to play devious? I'd perfected those skills when I'd been on the streets, begging for cash to score my next hit. Who knew I'd benefit from those now?

"What?" Don stared at me in disbelief that I'd interrupted him.

"The butler," I followed up quickly, knowing I had about ten seconds before that fist came smashing my way. "He brought a chest. Huge. It's important."

He held still. I exhaled a silent breath of relief. He was hooked. I could tell by the dilation of his eyes as greed slowly replaced rage. Now, I just had to reel him in. Too slow and I'd lose him. Too fast and he'd become suspicious. I had to play this just right.

"What's in it?" he asked.

"Remember that small chest of jewels?" I waited until he nodded. "Well, this chest is bigger. Twenty times bigger." Technically, I hadn't said this chest was filled with jewels, but then, that didn't really matter. I didn't mind lying to Don. I'd say anything to get him out of my car so I could go collect Jeremy and run.

Don pushed the car door open and stepped out

while lighting a cigarette. He didn't speak, he just paced back and forth, sucking his cancer stick, making me watch him take drag after drag. He knew it was a form of torture for me, that I hated things to drag out.

It worked.

By the time he finally flicked his cigarette onto the pavement, my nerves were frazzled.

"I'll take that chest, too. And if you don't deliver it all?" He stepped onto his cigarette and slowly ground it with his heel. "This will be Jeremy's head."

I swallowed. Whatever, Kass. Don't let him get to you. You just need to get out of here, get Jeremy and run.

"I'll need time," I said. I needed our trail as cold as possible before he even *thought* I'd run.

"I'm not unreasonable." He grinned. "A week?"

A week? In my dreams I couldn't have imagined him offering so much. I schooled my face into a look of outrage to throw him off track. "Not much time. This chest is bigger than the safe, Don."

He pounded the hood of my car with his fist. "A week. Don't get greedy."

"Fine," I snapped, reaching for my keys.

But Don didn't retire to his truck. Instead, in a flash, he was back in the passenger seat.

"What the hell?" I glared.

"Drive."

"Drive?" Shit.

Don pointed to the left. "I don't have all day. Drive."

What choice did I have? I edged the car around his truck and drove to the parking lot exit. "What are you—"

"My house," he said.

My heart sank. A lot of bad things had happened to me in Don's house. "What's wrong with your truck? Talk about not having all da—"

Don grabbed the back of my neck and squeezed. "My house."

There's no way his fingers weren't leaving a mark. Tears burned, but not because of the pain. The thought of me having to carry his bruises again dredged up so much of the past, the depression, the anger...the fear.

"Drive."

I did. I don't even recall the route I took. I just know about ten minutes later, I found myself parked in the driveway of Don's rundown split-level, set back a bit from the street.

Before I could react, he snagged the keys out of the ignition.

"Out," he barked as he exited the car.

Shit. I should have seen that coming. Wake up, Kass. You're not who you were. You're strong now. I clenched my jaw. Right. And if there was one thing I knew about Don, he fed off people's fear, sensing it like a shark does blood in the water.

I steeled my nerves, kicked back my door and stalked after him. "Give me my keys," I demanded, navigating across the yard filled with various motorcycles in stages of repair and decay and nearly tripping over a toilet with weeds growing out of it. How do toilets end up in people's yards? I've never understood that.

"Oh, you'll get them," he promised. He shoved his screen door open and took three steps inside before turning to dangle the keys over his head. "Come on then."

My every instinct screamed that going inside that house was a mistake. I stayed on the porch and planted my hands on my hips. "I'm tired of playing games. Give me the damn keys so I can finish the job."

He cocked his head to one side. "You don't want to see Jeremy then?"

My heart fell to my feet. I was inside the house

before he'd scarcely finished the last word. God. He'd taken Jeremy.

The door slammed shut behind me, and as I whirled, Don grabbed my wrist, crushing my bones in a vicelike grip.

"I thought you might pull this shit, you bitch, so I took out an insurance policy."

"What have you done to Jeremy?" I sobbed.

"Nothing...*yet*." He dragged me through the living room and down the narrow, dark hall. His carpet smelled like piss. "But I don't trust you. The game we're playing is gonna be mine and none of your bullshit."

He opened the bedroom door to the right and shoved me inside. I fought back, like my life depended on it, but Don was bigger, and in a battle of sheer muscle, he'd always win. Our confrontation ended quickly, with a punch to my jaw and a kick that sent me sprawling into a pile of dirty laundry in the middle of the room. Pain split my head, and the world around me spun. It took me nearly a minute to shove myself to my elbows, panting.

"Jeremy?" I gasped.

"Oh, Jeremy?" Don chuckled, crossing his arms. "He's not here. I lied."

Shit. *Shit.* "So much for your insurance policy, asshole." It was hard to talk. My jaw throbbed.

Don laughed, a real, deep belly laugh. "That's not the insurance policy. Believe me, you're in for a real treat."

I regained my feet and staggered toward the door, but he just shook his head, watching me and grinning. Then, when I was a few feet away, he stepped back, slammed the door, and twisted the key in the lock.

"No!" I screamed, rattling the knob, but it didn't budge. "You come back here, you miserable piece of shit!" I shouted, pounding the door with my fist until I could feel the bruises forming.

Don didn't answer.

I ran to the bedroom window and pulled the stained drapes aside, expecting to see a window I could open or break. Instead, I was greeted by a sturdy set of thick iron bars.

"There's no way out," a small, despondent voice whispered from behind me.

I froze.

I wasn't alone.

13

"Who's there?" I gasped, whirling in a circle as I searched the room. Boxes, clothes, and trash cluttered nearly every square inch of the place. Anything—or anyone—could be hiding in here. "Jeremy?"

I felt like a fool as soon as I said his name. The voice didn't sound like his at all, and Jeremy would've rushed straight at me or called my name.

When no one responded, I raised my voice a little louder, "Who is it?"

Again, nothing but silence.

Great. Now I was hearing things. I stayed by the window, feeling safer with a wall behind my back as I visually scoured the room.

Suddenly, the door flew back on its hinges and

166

Don strode inside, a small black bag in one hand and a bottle of Jack Daniels in the other.

I watched as he kicked a cardboard box off a white plastic lawn chair and took a seat.

"Want this?" he asked, balancing the bottle of Jack Daniels on his knee.

"Not interested." I wasn't. The thought of getting back on that addiction train made me sick. I just wanted out—and Don locked in a jail somewhere far away or maybe dumped in the middle of the Sahara Desert.

He dangled the small black bag and added, "Razors. For you." He tossed the bag and it landed at my feet.

I felt sick. "What are you up to? You can't kidnap me. They're going to miss me and—"

"Chill," he cut me short. "I'm not keeping you here for long. Let's just say that I'm detaining you until a few things happen. Part of the insurance policy."

"If you harm Jeremy in any way, you'll—"

"And why would I harm Jeremy now?" he asked, interrupting me again. "He's my guarantee, bitch. You'll walk to hell and back for him."

I clamped my mouth shut.

Don rolled his eyes, hefted himself off the chair

and stalked forward. He was quick, but then, I guess I just didn't have any fight left in me. I was too worried. I did push back, but he grabbed my hair and forced the bottle of whiskey into my mouth. God, I didn't want it, but my body did. A shudder rippled through me as the liquor rushed down my throat. I tried to shove the bottle back, to turn my head. I tried to fight, but I was gagging on the vile poison.

"Swallow," Don ordered. "Yeah, that's my girl."

I choked. I'd never be his. Then, as the warmth of the whisky coursed through my blood, I wasn't thinking about Don anymore. I hadn't had a drink in such a long, long time. Part of me felt sick. The other part wanted to grab the bottle from him and finish it off.

"No," I gasped, finally succeeding in wrenching myself away. "*Jeremy*. What have you done with him?"

"Nothing. Yet," he chuckled.

Don laughing was never a good sign. Then, something pricked my arm and I looked down to see Don holding a syringe.

"What the hell?" I gasped. I never did needles. Never.

"Good 'ol Oxycodone," he replied as he let me go. "You're gonna feel reaaal good in about twenty minutes, so you better get back. I'll follow. Just to make sure you get there in one piece. Can't have you missing all the excitement now, can we? And anyway, you've got a job to do."

I stared at him.

"Excitement?" I repeated hoarsely.

"I'll just get your keys, and then you're free to go." He paused at the door and looked back. "And don't think of detouring anywhere else. You want Jeremy? He's at the mansion. For now, anyway."

His words tore right through me. "What have you done?"

"Better trot on back to the Count and find out, huh?" he challenged. Then, he was out the door and I heard the click of the lock.

I lurched forward. I had to get to my phone. I must have left it in the car. I had to call Jeremy, warn him to stay hidden until I could get back.

"Let me go," a voice hissed from the mountain of clothing to my left.

I paused. God, what was it with me and clothing? Was I going to see them all start rising from the floor to dance around the room now?

I shook my head to clear it, the effects of the liquor and drugs already making my mind muddy.

"Here. I'm here."

Accompanied by the chinking of chains, a small, wizened creature, about three feet high, emerged from the mound of material. He looked old, grizzled, with a scrawny neck and a tuft of white hair that reminded me of those big-eyed troll dolls. His eyes were huge, too, much too large for his face.

"Let me go." The creature held up his hands, and at first, the only thing I could see was just how disproportionately large his hands were compared to the rest of his body. Then, he shook his wrists and I saw the manacles, big, iron ones, that bit into his flesh.

"What are you?" I whispered, unable to believe my eyes and quite convinced Don laced that drink or syringe with something hallucinogenic.

"A bog troll," he replied. "And I'll grant you a wish, anything you please, if you help me."

"A troll? Trolls don't grant wishes." Man, twenty minutes? I was already tripping.

"And how many trolls have you met?" the wizened creature challenged.

I snorted, pointed at him, and then blew imaginary smoke from my finger as if it were a gun. "You got me there." I chuckled. I felt strangely relaxed.

"Please," the bog troll whispered.

"Sure, I'll let you go." I met him halfway,

expecting him to vanish, but he didn't. He sure felt solid, as did his manacles. "Yeah, these aren't budging," I said, giving them a yank. "You need a key."

The bog troll wilted.

"It's ok," I patted him on the head. "You'll vanish soon enough and then you'll be free." I smiled at my own cleverness and then frowned. God, I was losing control. Jeremy. I had to focus but it was... So. Freaking. Hard.

The doorknob jiggled, signaling Don's return.

"Tell the Count I'm here," the troll hissed and then scurried back into the clothes pile.

"Sure thing," I agreed. I was feeling pretty good. Relaxed. I could still outwit Don. I just had to drive home, pick up Jeremy and skedaddle to Canada. Easy Peasy.

Don appeared out of nowhere. "Here are your keys."

I winced. "No need to shout," I grumbled as I grabbed them.

Then, I was in the driver's seat, wondering how I'd suddenly transported there.

"Does it matter?" I asked myself and then giggled.

I had to get home. For some reason. Oh, yeah. Jeremy.

"Right," I said, scowling in determination, but

then, I caught sight of my reflection in the rearview mirror. My pupils looked weird. So large. Kinda like that trippin' troll.

"Better start driving," Don's voice boomed through the window. "Shit, Kass. Don't pass out."

I saluted—with a middle finger—and then backed out of the driveway.

I don't remember much of the drive back to the mansion. It was dark and the oncoming headlights bounced around like beach balls. Several times, I swerved off the road.

Each time, Don appeared in my window, yelling at me to focus and get back. He kept shouting numbers at me. I floored the gas pedal, just to get away from him.

Then, I was pulling into the Count's driveway, or nearly, anyway. I saw the oncoming car at the last second and veered to the right, straight into the ditch.

My head smacked hard against the steering wheel as the car came to an abrupt stop.

The pain cleared the fog from my mind and gave me a moment of clarity.

Jeremy. I had to find him.

The coppery taste of blood filled my mouth as I opened the door and fell out of my car.

"Shit, bitch," Don was yelling at me. "Can't you do anything right?"

My nose throbbed in tandem with the punch Don had delivered to my jaw. I was a freaking mess.

"Jeremy," I whimpered.

"Well, you missed the fun," Don spat. He hooked his thumb over his shoulder. "That was him. In your dad's car. By now, they're halfway back home."

"No!" I gasped.

The terror in my voice made Don smile. "Oh, it'll get a lot worse for you, baby doll."

I clamped my mouth shut. He was pure evil. And evil had a lot of tricks.

"So, I have your attention now?" he asked.

He did, but he wouldn't for long. I felt a blackness rising up inside me. It was cold, like I imagined death would be.

He folded his arms and peered down at me, obviously getting off on tormenting me. "I'm saving Jeremy for last, for when I really need to punish you. In the meantime, you'll do what I say. You see, I've taken your precious brother away. Legally." He waved his phone in my face. "I'm turning your ass in for driving under the influence. Got the videos to prove it. When they arrive, they'll arrest you on the spot. Your dad will be all too happy to file a restraining order against you, and he'll have no problem getting one, not with the blood alcohol that *you'll* clock. Not to mention the drugs and kidnapping."

"*No*," I choked.

"They'll never give you custody after this. You've lost him now. And if you fail to get me that chest and the contents of that safe, you'll lose him for real. Permanently."

He kept talking, but the darkness rose to swallow me and I couldn't battle them both. All I could think about was Jeremy and the fact he was gone.

I ran down the driveway, screaming his name.

14

I don't know how, but suddenly, I was
bursting into the mansion. I couldn't
seem to stand up straight. The ground rolled in a
constant motion beneath my feet.

"Miss Kassandra?"

Leonard's long, narrow face floated before me,
and as I watched, his nose grew longer and longer,
until it had to be at least six feet long.

I frowned.

Something was wrong. Really wrong. But I
couldn't remember what, or how. In fact, I couldn't
remember anything.

Then, suddenly, the Count stood before me,
looking like a sculpted Greek god in a half-unbut-
toned shirt.

"Why just half undone?" I giggled, swaggering toward him. "Just take it all off. No silly fig leaves for *you*." I said, poking my finger into his muscled chest for emphasis.

The Count's dark eyes latched onto mine, and the more I stared into them, the more I began to feel the pain, taste the blood.

"What happened?" he asked, his deep baritone sounding so strangely far away.

What *had* happened? A jumble of thoughts crowded into my brain at that. Images of Don. A troll? My car in a ditch. Don's fist punching me in the jaw. All that alcohol…

Then, the blackness running beneath it all reared its ugly head once more, and suddenly I was tired. Just so. Damn. Tired. I was battling something, but I was too exhausted to figure it out anymore.

It was time to close my eyes.

"Kass," the Count's voice vibrated beneath my breasts.

Hmmm. I must have fallen? I didn't care. Not anymore.

"Don't go to sleep." This time, it was Leonard ordering me around. I liked him, but he wasn't compelling enough to keep me awake.

And anyway, I couldn't open my eyes. They were

too heavy. Just like it was too heavy to move my lungs to breathe.

I began to float, then. Or was it the Count running with me? I decided to go with that. It was much more exciting.

The next thing I knew, I lay on a bed. Candles surrounded me in a beautiful symphony of flickering light. The silk sheets felt so soft against my skin.

A body lay behind me, hard and strong. Warm lips suckled my neck, lips that pulled at my flesh in time with my beating heart. Lips that, with each passing second, drew me back from the blackness and into the candlelit realm surrounding me.

A different kind of haziness washed over me, a sensual one, and I moaned, arching back against chiseled chest and powerful thighs that cradled me.

The lips moved up the column of my throat and then over to nip the lobe of my ear.

"Like an instrument," the Count whispered.

I didn't think. I just reacted. I leaned back, pressing myself against him, wanting to feel every inch of his body connecting with mine. Safety. Lust. Understanding. I felt it all in his skin as it melded against mine. I didn't know how I'd gotten there, but I didn't care. I was there, where I belonged, and that was all that mattered.

He buried his nose against my skin and breathed deeply of my scent. "There's still more," he whispered.

As his palm outlined the curve of my hip, his mouth returned to my neck. I felt his teeth grazing my flesh, and a nip, like two needles, breaking the skin, and as he began to suck, I gasped in pleasure.

Never had I felt such heat running through me, pulsing with the need building in my core. I needed him. All of him.

Yet even as I began to writhe, pushing myself against his hardening flesh, images paraded through my head.

A dreamlike creature with troll hair.

My car in a ditch.

Don.

Hell, why would I want to think of Don now? I frowned and shoved him back into the recesses of my mind. But he wouldn't stay there.

The strange fuzziness in my thoughts began to clear.

I opened my eyes again. This time, I recognized my surroundings.

I was in the Count's room.

Naked.

On his bed.

God, he felt naked, too.

How had I ended up here? How freaking *unfair* to have forgotten such a thing?

But really, did it matter with the way his hot mouth pulled at the tender flesh at the side of my neck? I shuddered in pleasure with every sweep of his tongue.

I shifted beneath him, turning a little, enough to see his dark hair against my skin and the way the candlelight played over his rippling muscles. How erotic. I had to touch him. Feel him.

I slid my hand down, but the moment I touched his flesh, he lifted his head, surprised.

I froze, staring at his mouth.

His teeth were sharpened into a razor point and stained with my something red.

I reached for my own neck, feeling the sticky trail of blood, and suddenly all the pieces finally clicked together, completing the puzzle that had been the Count.

He doesn't eat.

He drinks only that strange, red wine.

He sleeps during the day and shuns the daylight within his home.

He has no heartbeat and doesn't show up on film.

And he has fangs and drinks blood.

179

I resisted the word that came to mind, knowing how insane it sounded, even to me.

But I couldn't deny what I was seeing with my own eyes, feeling with my own body.

I could blame the liquor and the drugs... that would make the most sense.

But I could feel the toxins leaving my body. My head was clearing. That's not how hallucinations worked for me.

That left me with one conclusion.

The Count was... a vampire?

And I was his meal.

y heart beat in my chest so loudly I couldn't hear the Count speak for a moment. His mouth moved, but the only sound I could hear was the panicked thumping.

"Why are we naked?" I looked around, trying to piece together the holes in my memory. A desperate fear teased the edges of my mind, but I couldn't remember why or what happened.

Our clothes lay in a folded pile on the iron-banded trunk at the end of the Count's massive four-poster bed. As I scurried off the satin sheets to reach for my shirt, a lock of wet hair flopped into my eyes.

"And why are we both soaking wet?" I asked, my gaze catching on the damp hollow in the mattress in the shape of our bodies.

The Count swung his feet off the bed. As he joined me at the trunk to shrug into his own shirt, I saw my blood, still staining his crimson lips.

"And what the actual hell?" I jabbered, fumbling with my jeans. God, it was like someone had duct taped the pant legs together. My body buzzed, and my mind leapt from one thought to another, but none of it made sense. "You're a vampire?"

The Count just stood there smirking. "Which question would you like an answer to first?" he asked softly, his voice sending shivers of pleasure through my traitorous body.

"I don't know," I shouted, my voice far too loud compared to his. "Just, tell me what the hell is going on."

Panic seized me, causing my heart to race, my vision to narrow, and my palms to sweat.

The Count searched my face and then with a frown, pulled me into his arms. "You're safe," he murmured into my hair, rubbing his hands up and down my back. "You're safe now."

I melted further into his chest, luxuriating in the feel of him even as I mourned the clothes that now created a wall between us. The memory of his body pressed against mine, skin to skin, melting me from the inside out. Part of me wanted to undress us both and crawl right back into bed together, staying there forever. But the rest of me knew I couldn't do that. I had to know what had happened.

Still, I stayed there in his embrace, tears stinging my eyes until I calmed enough to ask, "What happened?"

He brushed a stray lock of wet hair back from my face. "You showed up last night pumped full of drugs. You would have died from an overdose. I had to suck the poison out to save you."

Don. He'd kidnapped me. Kept me prisoner. Drugged me.

The car that almost hit me. My father. "Oh my God, Jeremy! My dad took him!" I attempted to pull away from the Count, but he held me closer still.

"Your brother is safe. I did not let that man take him. Leonard has been keeping an eye on him while I tended to you."

"Jeremy's here?" I asked, tears falling down my cheeks. "Safe?"

The Count nodded. "I swear it. I will not let harm come to him." He paused and then whispered, "Or you."

I froze, stunned by the longing and desire in his voice. Desire…for me? Emotion threatened to choke me, then the rest of what he'd said sank in. Overdose. "You saved my life?"

"Yes."

"But why were we naked? And wet?" I asked, not that I minded waking up naked with him, but if we were gonna get that sexy and shit, it would've been nice to remember it.

"You vomited all over both of us. I removed our clothing and put you in the shower to clean you up and help you gain some clarity. The latter goal failed, as you were too far gone, so I took you to bed to remove the drugs from your system." As he finished buttoning the last button of his crisp white shirt, he added, "Leonard cleaned our clothes, returned them, and here we are."

"I vomited on you?" Even as I asked the question a flash of a scene paralyzed me. Him carrying me in his arms up the stairs. Me trying to flirt, then puking all over us both.

He hadn't flinched or shown any negative reaction. He'd just continued up the stairs, gently undressed me, and rinsed me off.

Nothing untoward had happened, which was good... cuz I wanted to be of sound mind and body for any untoward action I was going to get with the Count.

Oh shit.

The vampire.

My boss was a vampire.

"You're a vampire."

A smile crooked the corner of his mouth. "Yes."

"So that's a thing. A real thing?" I'd seen his fangs. And they weren't the kind you could fake. But still, I had to ask.

"Yes."

"And Leonard?"

"Is not a vampire."

"But he's not human, is he?"

"No, not human, strictly speaking."

"So... you've killed people?"

He didn't hesitate. "Yes."

That was it. Just yes. No justification or apology. No trying to convince me he sparkled in the sun and only killed bad people. Just 'yes.'

"Are you going to hurt me or Jeremy?" I asked, biting my lower lip.

Again, he didn't hesitate. "I would kill to protect either of you."

"You say that now, but will you swear it? No matter what I tell you, do you swear you won't harm me or my brother?" I asked. Because I had to tell him everything. There could be no more lies between us.

185

He narrowed his eyes at me but nodded sharply. "I swear it."

I exhaled a breath I didn't realize I was holding in. "Then sit. I have a story to tell you."

He pulled me with him to the velvet tufted loveseat in front of the fire. If only I could just sit there with him. If only I didn't have to confess what I'd been up to. I knew by telling him the truth I was going to lose him. I just prayed I would survive it.

It took every shred of strength I possessed to face him, to begin. "I wasn't honest with you when I took this job," I confessed.

He raised an eyebrow but said nothing, waiting for me to continue.

"I was sent here to rob you." The words came out of my mouth like barbed explosives, landing between us and destroying anything that might have been growing there.

But I didn't hold back.

Didn't sugar coat it.

Didn't try to make myself look better than I am to him, just like I'm not making myself look better than I am to you.

He was as still as death while I spoke. Only when I got to the part about what Don did to me did he stiffen, his body tensed and readied itself like a panther on the prowl.

"Oh, and Don had a bog troll trapped in the house with me. I nearly forgot about all that with everything else that's happened," I added as an afterthought, and then I clamped my mouth shut to prevent myself from rambling any further. I was on the verge of babbling now, waiting for him to say something. Anything.

He remained silent for a very long time. The only sound in the room coming from the fire as the logs burned themselves down. I held my breath, worry and fear gnawing at me.

Then the Count stood abruptly and strode to a nearby chair to grab his black cloak draped over the back. When he reached the door, he turned to face me. "Don't leave the mansion."

And then he was gone.

I ran out of the room to stop him, to ask him what he was doing, to find out where we stood after all this, but he wasn't there. Just like before, he seemed to simply vanish and reappear out of thin air.

I ground my teeth in frustration, then dashed up the stairs to find Jeremy. I needed to see with my own two eyes that he was safe.

The door to our bedroom stood ajar, and I nudged it open.

On the floor in front of the fire, my brother sat across from Leonard, playing a board game. They were both laughing, Jeremy a full belly laugh and Leonard more of a dry chuckle. They stopped when I walked into the room.

"Kassy! You're okay!" Jeremy threw himself into my arms.

I hugged him fiercely and kissed the top of his head. "Hey, buddy. I'm fine." I pushed him back a little to get a better look at him. "Are you okay? Promise? This has been kind of a crazy night." That was an understatement, but I had no idea how much he knew. I had to proceed cautiously in order to not alarm him more than he already was.

His mouth took on a grim cast. "Dad showed up," he said softly, looking down at his feet before lifting his head and relaxing into a genuine smile. "But then Leonard scared him off and didn't even seem upset about how dad was acting. He's so cool. I want to be like Leonard when I grow up."

I snorted at that and glanced over at Leonard.

The butler looked slightly abashed at the compliment. Then, he turned his attention to my brother.

"You are already very brave. You need only strive to be more of yourself."

Jeremy puffed out his chest at that and dragged me to the board game, some kind of a fantasy quest saga. He handed me the mini princess sculpture and said, "I saved her for you to play. Come on. It's fun. We're about to fight the trolls."

I raised an eyebrow at that, thinking of the bog troll trapped by Don. And that only served to bring my thoughts back to the Count.

As if reading my mind, Leonard leaned over and asked quietly. "Where has he gone?"

I shrugged. "He didn't say, but he was pissed."

Leonard nodded as if it was all par for the course.

I eyed him curiously, wanting to ask him what he was, if not human or vampire... or troll, presumably. But with Jeremy right there, I knew it wasn't the right time. So, instead, I took my place on the floor before the fire and played the game.

I learned three things that night.

One: My brother was even more clever than I'd realized.

Two: Leonard was downright funny.

And three: My patience hadn't improved at all since I was a child.

It took everything in me to not pace the floor and wear a hole in the hardwood while waiting for the Count to return. Everything about my life and future lay at his feet and I hated not knowing what would become of us.

I tried to focus on just the positive, of having Jeremy safe and sound. I ruffled his hair just to have an excuse to touch him. Time passed. I rolled the dice and made my moves. Excited, Jeremy offered his opinions on how to play my character, sharing his strategies, but I only half listened.

My attention was more on the front door, downstairs.

It wasn't until an hour later—an hour that felt more like a year of sitting tense, every nerve raw with anticipation—that I heard the door open.

The sound sent me to my feet. "I have to go," I choked, my heart thumping loud in my chest. I glanced at Leonard. "Stay with him?"

The butler nodded.

"I'll be back, kiddo," I murmured to Jeremy, stroking his head one last time, just to remind myself that no matter what happened, it had all been worth it. "I just have to check in on the Count."

Jeremy nodded through his disappointment that I wouldn't be staying to finish the game, but he didn't argue. After all, the kid was used to being let down.

I raced downstairs, but the Count wasn't in the foyer. I found him in the kitchen, his back to the door, his long cloak stained with slashes of crimson.

Blood. My gut twisted.

"What happened?" I whispered, not sure I really wanted to know.

"I told you," he replied in a low voice without turning around. "I will kill to protect you and Jeremy."

My heart skipped a beat and my mouth went dry. "What did you do?"

He straightened and shifted his weight before turning to face me. "What needed to be done."

It took me a moment to register what he held in his hand.

When it clicked, I screamed.

The Count held a severed head, dripping blood onto the recently mopped kitchen floor.

And it wasn't just anyone's head.

It was Don's, his eyes still open, but empty of all life.

"You killed him?" I asked in a cracked whisper.

The Count eyed me, his handsome face an impassive mask. "This is who I am." He paused, and then dropped his voice to an even lower rumble to ask, "Who are you, Kassandra?"

16

I covered my mouth with my hands to stop from screaming even as I asked myself the same question. *Who was I?*

The answer snapped together in sharp relief as I stared at the decapitated head of the man who had tortured me for so long. And with each passing moment, the urge to scream faded away.

Who was I? I knew the answer to that. I really did. I stepped forward, only stopping before the Count when I was less than two feet away.

"I am a woman who can handle your darkness," I said, locking a fierce gaze with his. "That is, if you can handle mine."

At my response, a wealth of raw, naked emotion

played over the Count's face. Desire. Delight. And so many more.

He didn't move as I took Don's head from his grasp.

The hair felt greasy in my hands and the head weighed more than I'd imagined. I lifted it up, enough to stare into the dead eyes. Finally. It was over. I'd never have to hear his voice or deal with his sick cruelty ever again.

Relief bubbled inside me, along with years of pent anger. I'd suffered so much because of Don. I'd lived in such fear. Furious, I spat on his face and then tossed the head to the side, watching it roll along the tile until it thudded against a cabinet and came to a stop.

The Count lifted a cool brow, and then, he pulled me to him, and bending his head down, claimed my mouth with his own. I tasted blood on his tongue. Whose, I didn't know, nor did I care. I just let him sweep me away.

He kissed me with a rough possession, a kiss as fierce and dangerous as the man itself—well, not a man, but a vampire. The only kind of creature who could really match me, accept me as I was.

His tongue danced over mine, drawing me into his world in a kind of kiss that invited me to stay, and

I kissed him back with everything I had until I felt like I would burst.

God, I belonged with him.

I ran my hands over his hard-muscled chest and then wanting to feel his skin against mine, pulled his shirt free enough to slip my hands beneath.

He moaned into my mouth as I ran my palms up his spine, marveling in the soft, satiny coolness that covered muscle as hard as rock.

He answered my exploration with one of his own, sliding his hands down over my hips to cup my ass and pull me, sharply, against him.

He was hard. I arched against him, wanting more this time.

"Stay with me," he groaned, thrusting his hips forward to meet me.

"Forever," I promised in a whisper.

He blanched at my response, and for a sick moment, I thought he'd pull away, that I'd ruined the heat sizzling between us. Forever? Why was that such a trigger word?

I threaded my fingers through his hair and pulled his head down to kiss him desperately, letting him feel the need inside me. I kissed him with everything I had.

He relaxed and gathered me back in his arms, this

time, holding me gently, as if I might break. Then, he hefted me onto the granite island, the difference in height allowing him to bury his face against my throat.

I closed my eyes and let my head fall back as he kissed the line of my collarbone, making his way to the vein on my neck.

When his fangs grazed my skin, I felt no fear. Instead, the touch sent shivers through my every nerve, kindling a heat, deep inside me. A heat that demanded I had to have him.

Now.

I didn't care what he might think. I tugged at his cloak, sending it to the floor, and then I attacked his shirt, ripping a few of the buttons impatiently, wanting to again feel every inch of him pressed against mine.

He did a far better job with the shirt ripping. In one smooth motion, he had mine off entirely. My bra quickly followed.

"Like an instrument," he murmured against my neck, and then, his mouth descended in a slow, lazy inspection that left a trail of fire until finally, his mouth closed over my breast.

"God, don't stop," I gasped as he suckled, each pull driving me into a hotter frenzy.

I held his head tight against me, playing with his hair as he teased me, alternating his tongue with tiny pricks of his fangs. *This* was what I'd been looking for while cutting. The sheer amount of emotion, of feeling. After this, I'd never cut again.

Then, he was pushing me back against the granite, flat on my back. The stone felt cool beneath my skin as he unzipped my jeans and peeled them off my legs so easily, leaving me in nothing but my panties, a red lacy thong.

That fact summoned a wealth of disappointment, but before I could give voice to my dissatisfaction, he stepped between my legs and dropped his mouth against the tender flesh of my inner thigh.

Slowly, he kissed each of my scars, taking his time, and then, his fangs skimmed along my veins, up and ever up, until his tongue slid so slowly, so torturously, beneath the lace of my thong.

I gasped.

I didn't last long under that gentle assault. He nibbled and nipped, and I could do nothing but lay on the granite, clutching his head in my hands as his tongue drove me to the brink of sweet madness and then beyond.

I came, harder than I ever have, the strength of

my orgasm sending me nearly off the kitchen island. He rose to hold me tenderly.

"I want you," he breathed in my ear as I collapsed against him.

He wanted me. *Me*. What did that say, after all I'd done? That I was worth being loved?

The thought made it hard to breathe.

"For me, this will be forever," he continued, nuzzling my neck.

"Me too," I said, never meaning it more, even as part of me, deep inside, wondered if his version of 'forever' meant something more than the normal wordplay between lovers.

Then, I heard him unbuckle his belt and as his pants slid to the floor, all other thoughts faded away. I could only feel, experience every nuance of sensation his mouth summoned as it explored me, teasing me again into a passionate, heated fever.

He took me there, against the island. Hard and powerful, raw. A master, balancing me easily in his arms until this time, we both came together.

Afterwards, he held me close for a time, in complete silence. Then, still in silence, he carried me up the steps to his room, so quickly that to all other eyes, we were but a blur.

"You are mine," he rumbled, laying me gently on the satin sheets. "You're mine. Wanted. Forever."

Our passions lasted all night, never fully satiated no matter how many times we each climaxed together. His stamina was endless, as endless as my need for him, my desperate need to feel him inside me. As one last orgasm crashed through me, his teeth sunk into my neck, and the balance of pleasure and pain made me lose my mind in the best possible way.

After, we lay together, my head on his chest, his arms wrapped possessively around me, my left leg intertwined with his as my body curved against him. I traced the contours of his chest, breathing in the scent of him, the gift of him.

"Shit!" I said, looking up at him as a sudden realization dawned on me.

"What is it?" he asked, his voice heavy with our recent escapades.

"It just occurred to me I don't even know your name."

His lips curved up into a smirk. "Some might say confessing eternity to someone whose name you do not know is folly."

I stretched up to kiss his chin. "What is a name anyways? It doesn't change the nature of a thing. I know you. But it would be helpful to also know your name."

"Vlad Dracule," he said softly. "But that name comes with a lot of history, much of it I'd rather forget."

"Vlad Dracule?" I asked, my mind sifting through the stories and lore. "Like, as in Dracula? You were named after Dracula?"

When he didn't respond, the truth slammed into me and I gasped, sitting bolt upright. "Not named after Dracula," I clarified, the puzzle completing in my mind. "You *are* Dracula? Vlad the Impaler? All the stories?"

He nodded, his narrowed eyes watching my every move. "I am. Though the stories are not all true." He paused noticeably, before adding, "The truth is much worse. I am much worse."

His words contained no self-pity, just unvarnished truth. He wanted me to see him, the real him. He'd showed me his truth when he'd brought me Don's head. Now, from the way he studied me, I understood he needed to know if I could handle the full impact of his history, as well.

I slid back into the sheets and propped myself up on his chest so I could see his face better. Then, caressing his cheek, I held his gaze with mine. "You can call yourself whatever you want. You can be whoever you want. I love you as you are. You don't have to hide from me."

His eyes flickered wider, then he cupped my face, sliding a finger down my jawline. "You are most extraordinary, Kassandra. You have me. My love. My eternal devotion. I will always stand by you."

My heart swelled with his words, reshaping my inner landscape from the barren wasteland I always imagined it to be to something fertile and ripe with new growth. His love planted within me nourished my soul in a way nothing else had ever done. I was his. He was mine. Nothing could tear us apart.

"What would you like me to call you?" I asked.

"Vlad," he said. "You can call me Vlad."

I smiled. "It's a good name. It suits you."

We spent the rest of the night talking. Sharing our stories, our pain, our triumphs. He told me more about his wife, her death, their child. It ripped open my heart, seeing him so vulnerable.

"I loved her," he confessed softly, "but it was an incomplete love. She could never accept the darkness inside me. I tried to change for her, to be more human, but that wasn't in me to give her."

"You don't need to change for me," I reminded him. "I accept you as you are."

I knew as we talked that I would never know everything about him. He had lived too many lives to ever encapsulate that into mere words. But I got to know the essence of him. His hopes and dreams. His loves and losses.

As we finally fell asleep in each other's arms, there was only one question I didn't dare ask. One thought that haunted me and made me wonder.

He had wanted a child so badly he married a human and she had died.

He never turned her.

Had he planned to? Or had he been content to let her live her mortal life to its completion?

And what did that mean for me? Would he want me to become like him? A vampire? So we could live together forever? Or did our love have an expiration date. Would he want me to stay human?

And what did *I* want from all this?

Was I ready to give up my humanity—and daylight—for an eternity with him?

As soon as I thought the question, I knew the answer.

Yes.

Humanity had never done much for me anyways, and the sun was overrated.

I wanted to be like him. I wanted to become a vampire.

But would he want to make me one?

That's the question I was scared to ask.

Because if he said no, that meant our time together was finite.

And that broke the fragile hope growing with me.

I needed forever with him.

Nothing less would ever do.

17

When I woke, I could tell it was daylight outside. The Count—Vlad—slept deeply by my side, our limbs entangled, his body, even in sleep, primed and ready for another round of lovemaking. I gazed with longing at this beautiful being I would spend my life with and wondered at all that had happened since I came to this mansion.

I was still in shock how easily he'd accepted my confessions. I truly expected him to flip the hell out, and if not kill me outright, certainly kick my butt to the curb.

But instead, he'd brought me my enemy's head.

That should have freaked me out, but it didn't. It made me feel loved.

Maybe that made me sick, but I didn't care. It made us a match, and I was happier than I could ever remember being.

He eased my emotional pain and made me feel alive in a way nothing else had, not even cutting. Looking at him now, I knew I wouldn't need my razors anymore. Not with him in my bed, inside my body and soul. He had woken up the dormant part of me and injected me with a life unlike any other.

Reluctantly, I slid out of bed, in desperate need of the bathroom, a shower, and coffee. My body ached pleasantly as I took care of my morning business— though at this point, it was probably late afternoon.

The hot shower eased some of the tenderness created by a vigorous night of lovemaking, and I couldn't help but smile as I recalled the details of being with him. It took everything I had not to crawl back into bed to see how deeply he actually slept during the day, but instead, I dressed in one of his t-shirts and a pair of sweats and headed downstairs for coffee.

I grabbed my phone on the way, checking missed calls, and sighed. Over twenty-three. Two from Don —pre-beheading, obviously, the rest from my father. The sight of Don's number made me think of the head in the kitchen, and I realized I had to clean it up before Jeremy woke. God, if he was already up, the sight of Don's head would send him to therapy for the rest of his life.

But when I entered the kitchen, it was spotless. Not a drop of blood, and no sign of severed heads.

Leonard had clearly gotten here first. Bless that man, whatever he was.

I did, however, notice the large chest he'd brought back from his trip stood in the corner of the kitchen by the pantry.

As the housekeeper, it would be inappropriate to snoop.

As Vlad's... what was I? His girlfriend? Lover? Mate? At any rate, my role had changed overnight, so that had to change the rules, right?

Justifying my curiosity, I lifted the lid an inch to peek inside.

Black smoke billowed out at once, in tendrils that looked like long, dark curling fingers. Startled, I slammed the lid shut, my heart pounding in my chest.

And then I laughed. I laughed because what else can you do when you fall into an alternate reality where vampires are real and shadow creatures live in boxes in your kitchen? This was my life now, and as mildly terrifying as it was, it was even more exhilarating. Adrenaline pumped through my veins as all the possibilities of my new life settled into me.

I was untouchable.

Don was dead.

My father couldn't hurt me anymore.

Jeremy would be safe.

A giddy relief washed over me and even when my phone rang and I saw my father's number appear, my mood didn't change.

A new courage took hold, and I answered the call with a confidence born of blood and death.

"Where the hell is my son?" my dad said, his voice slurred from alcohol.

"You don't get to talk to me like that anymore," I informed him, no longer scared of this weak, pathetic man.

"I can talk however the hell I want. Bring Jeremy home, or I'll send the cops your way."

I just laughed. "Your cop buddies think you're a joke, you know that, right? They talk shit about you behind your back. They mock your drunk ass and they're relieved you're no longer on the force."

I didn't know if what I said was true, but it didn't really matter. My words were venomous arrows that found their mark in my father's fragile ego, shattering pieces of it.

After clamping the troll's hands together, he wrapped the chain around the bedpost. Obviously, that bog troll wasn't going anywhere.

"There." My father dusted his hands together in a job well done.

He grabbed a Bud Light, popped the tab, and chugged the beer down all in one go. I could hear him swallow all the way from the closet. When he'd finished, he tossed the can in the general direction of the trashcan, belched, and then folded his arms to squint down at the bog troll.

"Name?"

"Sam," the troll whined.

"How many aliases have you got?" my dad demanded, slamming his fist down on his desk. "That's the fifth name you've given me."

"Kind sir, I'll go by any name you wish," the pathetic creature whimpered.

My heart tugged. I had to rescue the little guy. But how?

My father muttered something under his breath and then, a bit unsteadily, turned back to his desk and began searching through the piles of paper. Maybe after a few more beers, he'd pass out and I could rescue the troll and take him back to Vlad.

Surely, Vlad would know how to help him get back home?

The troll quivered on the bed, his large eyes focused on my father as he bumbled around, still muttering and clearly looking for something.

But then, as he bent down to search under the desk, the troll on the bed changed. The trembling vanished. The large eyes narrowed into murderous slits. The mouth opened and grew wide, revealing several large rows of teeth.

I blinked in shock.

As the troll leaned toward Dad, straining against the chains, my father suddenly straightened.

"Here it is," he said, turning to brandish a flat black Glock 20.

At the sight of the gun, the troll melted back, adopting a subdued demeanor.

I stared. So, the troll wasn't as helpless as he seemed.

"You'll show respect for the law," My father growled, grabbing another beer while waving the gun in his other hand. With an expertise born of years of one-handed practice, he popped the tab of his beer with his finger while still holding the can. He slurped a swig and pointed the gun in the troll's face. "You'll tell me what I want to know. Don said you knew all about the goings on in the Count's house. Now, spill it, Sam, Fred, Jack or whatever the hell your name really is."

The troll? So, the troll was how Don had gotten all his inside information?

"Let me go, and I'll grant your wish," the troll wheedled, his eyes as round as an owl's. There wasn't a hint of those many rows of teeth, now. "Let me go, and I'll hand over not only your son, but your daughter, too. She'll be yours to control. Forever." His mouth widened into a malicious grin.

The little *shit*. Any sympathy I had for him died that instant.

"If you're lying, you'll pay with your miserable life," my dad grunted. He guzzled his beer and then crumpled the can.

"The Count is rich, and your daughter has the codes," the troll cackled. "When you control her, she'll get it all for you. She'll be yours to command. For everything."

He was willing to sell me out for his own benefit, was he? Well, Vlad would have something to say about that—when I could get out of here to tell him.

"So, that's what she's been up to," my father belched. "Getting rich and letting her old man suffer."

Where had all the 'by the law' crap gone now? Funny how his principles flew out the window the moment money was mentioned.

"You'll tell me how to get inside that mansion." My dad turned on the troll.

"You can't just break in there," the troll said with scowl. "The Count is not of this world. He's to be feared."

No shit. And just wait until he heard what was really happening.

"He's nothing I can't handle," my dad bragged with a belligerent shrug.

I doubted that. Part of me was tempted to step out of my hiding place and egg my dad into coming at Vlad. It would be problem solved, then, but as dark as I was, I knew I never would. I didn't want to directly cause his death. I'd settle for scaring him away, permanently, letting karma handle the rest. After all, the way he was going, there'd be a big boomerang of karma soon, judging by the law of statistics.

"It's a deal then," the bog troll grinned. It wasn't a happy kind of grin, but a slimy one, the kind con artists wear when they've achieved their goal. "I'll give you the power to enter his house, if you let me go."

"Power?" My dad repeated, knitting his brows in confusion. "The security codes?"

Oh, Dad. You have no idea what you're getting yourself into.

"Power," the bog troll nodded eagerly, as if that would hypnotize my dad into agreeing. "You want your son? I'll give you a potion, you'll get powerful. No one will stand in your way, then."

"You don't say," My father belched, reaching for another beer.

"Guaranteed."

"Deal, then. Let's see what you got."

"Let me go, first."

That triggered my father into pressing the gun against the troll's temple. "I'm not stupid. Give me the potion, first. I'll not have you escape without holding your end of the bargain. Don warned me about you."

The troll's eyes narrowed into slits again. "A knife and a cup," he spat. "We'll make an even trade. I'll hand you the cup and you'll hand me the keys." He held up his cuffed wrists and then pointed at the chain around his neck.

"Deal," my dad agreed.

I stifled a snort. Why do criminals ever trust other criminals? I've never understood that. And anyone who'd believe a word out of my dad's mouth was a fool.

"Here," my dad said, tossing a penknife on the bed before retrieving a red plastic Solo cup from the floor that hadn't made it into the overflowing trashcan. "Where's this potion?"

The troll sniffed, but grabbed the knife, sliced his finger and squeezed a few drops of black blood into the cup.

A rancid stench filled the room.

"You want me to drink that shit?" My dad snorted when the creature held up the cup.

I gagged at the thought. But honestly, I didn't really care what they did. They could play their games, con each other, it didn't matter. Karma would bite their asses, and if they showed up at my house looking to start shit, Vlad would bite more than that.

The sound of chains falling to the floor snapped my attention back to the present. They'd made the exchange, and my dad was apparently drunk enough to drink the foul-smelling blood. As I watched, he splashed a little beer into the cup, swished it around and brought it to his lips.

The troll huddled at the foot of the bed, twisting the key into the handcuff lock. He fumbled, his hands too large, and dropped the key. Swearing, he reached for it and tried again.

My father straightened and set the empty cup down on a pile of case files. "Interesting," he said, his voice sounding unusually deep.

The troll grinned as the handcuffs finally fell away. He was off the bed and out the door in a flash.

And my dad, who moments ago could barely stand upright, now charged out of the room after him, quicker than I'd ever seen him move in my life.

What the hell had been in that troll's blood? Didn't matter. This was my chance to escape, now or never. With the raucous those two were making, I didn't worry about stealth. Speed mattered more at this point. I tore out of the closet faster than any hound of hell could ever dream of running.

I flew into the hall, but instantly skidded to a halt.

My dad stood at the end of the hall, his gun pointed at the bog troll as the creature made a dash for the front door.

Shit. He'd cut off my escape. I'd have to return to my dad's bedroom and hope the window wasn't still stuck. And while it was in the opposite direction, it was a long hallway that would leave me exposed for far too long.

Before I could make up my mind, the gun went off, the shot so loud, my ears rang.

Shocked, I turned back towards my dad to see the troll lying on the floor in a crumpled heap—like a bag of trash left on a curb.

My dad leapt forward with animalistic dexterity to crouch beside the creature's limp body, and then with a growl that sounded like a feral wolf, he bit the troll's neck.

I stared, unable to move. Had my father somehow turned into a vampire? That made no sense.

He attacked the creature's flesh, guzzling the blackened blood with a great smacking of the lips, the stench of it filling the house and causing my stomach to clench. Bile filled the back of my throat and I knew I would lose the contents of my stomach if I didn't get out. Now.

No matter if he saw me or not. I took off down the hall at full speed, but halfway to the door, I heard him.

"Kass, I'm coming for you," my father called after me. His voice had changed and had a layered dual tone that sent a new kind of fear creeping down my spine.

What the hell kind of voice was *that?* He sounded downright demonic.

I knew I should just keep running, but I didn't. I stopped and turned. Maybe it was curiosity at the change in his voice. Maybe, just like the bog troll had promised, he could control me now.

Whatever it was, I turned around. I had to see.

My father hadn't moved. He still crouched on the floor, the troll's limp body in his arms. Blood dripped down his chin and onto his clothes as he smiled at me.

But then, I saw them.

His eyes.

They were glowing.

18

I flew out of the house and down the block. My hands shook so bad it took me five tries to jam my keys into the ignition. I kept looking all around, expecting at any moment to see my father running towards me like the devil himself.

At last, the car started, and I peeled out of there, speeding through the neighborhood streets until I was out of town and zooming down the highway.

I had to tell Vlad. He'd know what to do.

My father was enough of a nightmare before this extra dose of evil infected him.

The day was nearly spent, the sun sinking beneath the line of trees as I drove.

Technically, it wasn't night yet. Would Vlad be

awake, or was he the kind of vampire that only woke as that last splash of sunlight faded in the sky?

There was still so much I didn't know, didn't understand, about this new world I'd stumbled into. When this shit with my dad was over, I would be peppering Vlad with a shit ton of questions.

I was nearly at the mansion when my car sputtered, and I realized it was on empty. Shit, shit, double shit.

I willed my car on, as if my thoughts could power it in lieu of gas.

The car gods smiled upon me, and I made it to the driveway before my car ground to a halt with no more fumes left to power it.

I nearly tripped running into the house, my breath coming in spurts, my lungs burning as I flew up the stairs and crashed through Vlad's bedroom door.

He lay on the bed just as I'd left him.

"Vlad," I gasped, diving onto the sheets beside him.

He didn't move. He lay there, still as a corpse.

I shook him, hard.

Nothing.

In desperation, I pummeled his chest. "Wake up!"

Still nothing.

Shit. Shit. Shit.

How was I going to deal with my demon dad if he showed up before Vlad woke?

Abandoning him, I ran to Jeremy's room, shoving open the door.

The room was empty.

"Jeremy!" I screamed, leaving his room and running downstairs.

Where would a growing boy be if not in his room? The kitchen.

I found him there, kneeling before the black chest Leonard brought home.

The lid was open and whatever black smoke had been there before seemed to have escaped.

That was probably a bad thing. "Jeremy, what are you doing?"

He looked up at me, his eyes shadowed. "What's wrong?"

"You shouldn't be messing with that trunk," I said, worry and anxiety warring within me. I had no idea what the trunk contained, but I didn't have time to deal with it now.

He looked down sheepishly. "Sorry."

"It's okay, buddy. But I need you to stay close to me." I headed for the block of knives and selected the largest one. I had to defend us. At least until sunset.

"What happened?"

"It's Dad," I said. "He's not normal anymore."

"Was he…ever?" Jeremy asked nervously.

"Well, he's worse now," I said grimly. "Like he's on some kind of drugs." Bog troll blood could be considered a drug. Didn't account for the glowing eyes, though. "We just have to wait a few minutes. The sun will set soon. Then, Vlad will be here."

"Vlad?"

"The Count," I sighed. Now was as good a time as any to introduce Jeremy to his new reality. He had to know. Now. Especially if Dad showed up at the door with fangs and glowing like he'd been dipped in radiation.

I explained it all, as fast and gently as I could.

Jeremy took the news well. Maybe too well. "Dracula?" he repeated, his face splitting into a wide grin. "*The* Dracula?"

I nodded; not sure he was taking this the right way. "It's—"

"Freaking *awesome*."

I scowled. "I was going to say dangerous."

"What is this?" Leonard stood at the kitchen door looking at his wooden chest, his narrow face angry, his clipped voice harsher than I've ever heard him. "Who opened this? How?"

I didn't have time for this. "We're sort of dealing with an emergency—"

"This is important," Leonard cut me short.

The fact that he'd interrupted me clamped my mouth shut. Leonard was always the gentleman, so polite.

"I did," Jeremy surprised me by saying. "I heard them whimpering. They wanted to play."

"Them?" I asked, on edge and still clutching my knife in my sweaty palm.

Leonard's brows rose to his hairline.

"What has happened?" The Count's cool baritone sliced through the tension in the room.

"Vlad!" I exhaled in relief, the death grip on my knife loosening as I rushed to him.

He pulled me into an embrace, his arms encircling me. I breathed in his scent—an intoxicating blend of old parchment, sandalwood and smoke—and it calmed my racing heart.

"The boy has released the Shadows," Leonard said.

"How is that possible?" Vlad asked, his chest rumbling as he spoke.

"There is only one explanation," Leonard replied, his voice filling with wonder.

Vlad inhaled and lifted a curious brow in Jeremy's direction. "Fascinating. The Shadows choose so few."

I reluctantly pulled away from Vlad's embrace. "What are the Shadows?" I asked. "And could they help defeat someone who was high on troll blood?"

Vlad stiffened, his gaze landing on me. "Why do you ask?"

"Remember that bog troll I told you about?" I asked in turn. "The one Don was keeping prisoner?"

Vlad nodded, waiting patiently for me to continue.

"Well, I went to his house to find the blackmail videos he took, and the troll was gone. Then I went home—"

"That was not wise," Vlad interrupted, his jaw muscles tensing. "I cannot protect you during the day. Not in this world."

Whoa. Okay, there was a lot to unpack in that casually thrown out sentence. Not in this world? What other worlds were there? Another question to add to growing list once we made it out of this mess.

"I couldn't just sit around doing nothing. I needed to collect dirt on my dad so I can get proper custody of Jeremy," I explained.

Vlad's eyes narrowed, but he didn't respond, so I continued.

"While I was there, my dad showed up. With the bog troll in tow. I'm assuming he got him from Don's house. Anyway, the troll was chained up and made a deal with my dad for his freedom."

The Count snorted. "They're disgusting creatures. And their magic is weak, short-lived. Con artists, the lot…for the most part."

My dad's glowing eyes begged to differ. "He offered a vial of his blood for his freedom."

The Count tensed beside me, and I glanced at Jeremy to see how he was handling this. He wasn't paying attention and seemed distracted by something on the floor. When I glanced at his feet, I noticed black shadows curled around his ankles, like puppies.

"What?" I gasped.

Leonard followed my gaze and his jaw dropped.

"Did your father drink the blood?" Vlad asked, breaking my focus on Jeremy's new friends.

I nodded. "It changed him. He grew stronger, faster, more deadly."

"And where is the troll now?" Vlad asked, his voice unnaturally calm.

Leonard began whispering something to Jeremy, and it was hard to concentrate on the Count's questions with the way the Shadows were splitting up, dividing themselves between my brother and Leonard. What the hell was going on?

"Kassandra?" Vlad prompted, an edge of steel entering his tone.

"Um, the troll? My dad chased him down and shot him, he—"

"Did the troll die?" Leonard asked suddenly, his attention momentarily diverted from the shadows swirling around his feet.

"Yes," I said. "And then… " I swallowed the lump in my throat. "Then my dad fed on him, like a vampire."

I studied Vlad's face for any reaction, but he carried all of his emotions in a clenched jaw.

"Not a vampire," he objected softly. "A chimera."

"Chimeras are real, too?" Jeremy asked, his voice way too excited.

"I thought they were Greek myths," I said, trying to remember what little I'd heard about the creatures.

"You also thought I was myth until recently," Vlad whispered in my ear, slipping an arm around my waist.

My pulse sped up in response to his proximity and I leaned into him, my body acting of its own accord. How did he manage to arouse me even at the most inappropriate time?

He smirked as if he could tell what I was thinking.

Brain, focus.

"Tell me about chimeras," I said, deliberately shifting away from the Count's sexy-ass body.

His gaze roved over me a few seconds before he replied, "Chimeras are powerful, demonic creatures made when someone without magic feeds on the life-force of one with dark magic, such as a bog troll. All magical beings are created from one of the six elements. Earth, air, fire, water, light and darkness. If a human consumes the dark soul of a magical being, they become a demon. They become a chimera."

My dad had basically been a demon before the bog troll. I shuddered to think what he'd turned into, now.

"Can you stop him?" I asked, uneasy.

"Yes." Vlad's nod was firm, confident. "But it won't be easy. Especially this soon after his transformation. He'll be at his most powerful. And likely he is already feeding, increasing his strength. We need to find him and stop him."

"No," I said. My eyes fell on Jeremy and I added grimly, "We don't need to find him. He'll find us."

Vlad clenched his fist and when Leonard met his

glance, they nodded in a shared understanding. "Then we'll be ready." Vlad turned to leave.

I stepped forward and grabbed his hand, intertwining my fingers with his. "Where are you going?"

"To the forge," he said, giving my fingers a squeeze.

I'd pretty much forgotten about the fact the mansion had a forge. "Then I'm coming with you." I glanced over my shoulder to where my brother sat at the kitchen island. "Stay inside with Leonard, okay?"

I hated leaving him, but I needed to talk to Vlad alone, and this might be my only chance.

Jeremy nodded as I left the kitchen hand in hand with the Count. "What did you wish to speak to me about?" Vlad asked as we left the mansion through a back entrance and headed through the gardens to the forge.

The night was cool with a fresh breeze carrying the scent of roses and a dark sky full of stars, lit by a full moon.

"How did you know I wanted to talk about something?" I asked, tucking myself closer to him.

"You get a certain look," he said.

On any other night, this would feel romantic. A stroll through the rose garden under a full moon. But tonight, it felt too threatening, too sinister to relax into, but still, every moment with Vlad felt magical.

I paused and led him to a bench where we both sat.

"I do have something to say," I said as he stiffened, watching me with suddenly suspicious eyes.

I sucked in a breath, trying to find the right way to approach this. I was so nervous I had to wrench the words out of my throat with force. "I want you to turn me," I said, finally.

His eyes widened and then he laughed.

Like straight up laughed.

Like full belly laugh.

I pulled back, tears stinging my eyes. I didn't know what I'd expected, but him mocking me certainly hadn't been it.

I rose to my feet, hiding my face. I didn't want him to see how much hurt his laughing had caused. So, I was a joke to him. Not a forever love, but rather a momentary lay. Clearly, his declarations of love were just a seduction ploy. He probably said them to all the women he took to bed.

But I took no more than two steps before he grabbed my hand and pulled me unto his lap.

I stiffened, no longer content to play the convenient lover role. "Let me go," I growled, fighting the tears.

"Why are you angry?" he asked, sounding confused.

"I'm just a joke to you. A toy."

"Is that what you think?" He shook his head.

"Isn't that why you find the idea of turning me into a vampire so hilarious?"

He cupped my face, his gaze penetrating mine. "I thought you were about to tell me you'd had enough, that this life was too dangerous for you and you wanted out. And you would be right. If I was less selfish I would push you away. Out of this world of danger and magic." He paused and then smiled, a tender smile. "But I can't let you go. I laughed out of relief. I never imagined you would want to become a monster, to be with, and love, a monster like me."

The breath I didn't realize I'd been holding left me in a rush, to be replaced by a bone-deep relief. "So…" I hesitated and the asked, "You don't want to get rid of me?"

He chuckled softly.

"Woman, did you not hear any of the words I spoke to you last night? I want you forever. You are mine."

I slipped my arms around his neck, and he pulled

me into a deep kiss that crashed through my body, sending waves of pleasure that left me breathless, intoxicated, and in desperate need of more.

As he trailed kisses down my chin, onto my neck, I melted into him.

"You want to become a vampire?" he whispered against my skin.

"Yes. I want to be with you forever," I said. "And I want to be stronger. Faster. More powerful."

"You would be giving up a lot," he warned, his hands sliding down my back to cup my ass.

"I would be gaining so much more," I countered, moaning a little as his teeth grazed my skin, teasing at the pulsing vein.

"You won't be able to have children. Or enjoy the sun." His voice softened at this, making me realize he considered those his greatest losses.

"We have Jeremy. He can be our child," I whispered back. "And you are my sun."

His breath hitched at that, and I felt his arousal beneath me as he pressed closer still.

"It will hurt," he said finally, his teeth pressing against my flesh.

"Trust me, I can handle pain."

Then he pierced me and began to suck.

I didn't know what to expect beyond what I'd seen and read in pop culture.

I prepared for pain, but a euphoric pleasure pulsed through me as I became lightheaded from blood loss. I don't know how long that lasted, but when he finally supported me in his arms and slit his own wrist open with his teeth, I hovered on the brink of consciousness.

"Drink," he said, holding the dripping blood over my mouth.

I felt parched, desperate for what he offered, and I drank deeply, my eyes closed, my body limp in his embrace. But with each mouthful, I began to change. He filled me with his lifeforce. I could feel the magic working, transforming me. Making me stronger.

Then, the pain hit.

Everything turned black as I screamed into the night, my body writhing, my mind splitting into pieces as time stretched before me into eternity. All I knew was pain. There was no other reality, and in that never-ending moment, I prayed for death.

19

*G*radually, the pain faded. I felt so drained, I couldn't even lift my eyelids. Time passed.

Finally, I became aware of the Count's arms, locked around me, cradling me close to his chest.

I just stayed there, unmoving, keeping my eyes closed.

I noticed a heightened sense of smell, first. A warmth on the wind. Something I could only describe as 'life.' Instinctively I knew what it was. Jeremy's warm blood, coming from inside the house. I could smell Leonard, too, whatever he was.

Startled, I lifted my eyelashes.

The world around me looked so different. Beautiful. Alive. The darkness lending a different dimension of color I never knew existed. I could see life in shades of neon. The energy coursing through the trees, traces of blue and green running through the veins of the leaves.

Above, the moon glistened bright, as if it were its own kind of sun. And the darkness of the sky seemed to almost shine its own black version of light.

I stirred in Vlad's arms, wrapped so tight about my waist, so gently. The empathy in his eyes nearly undid my soul.

"The pain will not come again," he whispered, pressing his cheek against mine. "As long as you stay out of the sun."

I studied his face easily in the dark, seeing every line of concern on his brow. Clearly, he feared I'd regretted my choice. I smiled and traced the line of his jaw with a fingertip. "What need have I for that sun when I have you?"

He peered back at me from hooded eyes. "When you are stronger and have fed, I will show you the true beauty of the night."

I sighed, wishing he could show me now, but I knew better. We had to defend ourselves from whatever demon now inhabited my father's body.

It was strange. I guess now that meant he was dead. The thought brought nothing but relief. I couldn't even force a tear, not with the pain and torture he'd caused, yet, I did feel an odd sense of sorrow. I guess for the loss of what he could have been.

"Come." Vlad held out his hand.

I followed him to the forge, a stone outbuilding complete with an anvil, fireplace, and bellows.

"What are you doing?" I asked as Vlad began selecting tools from the various hooks on the wall: tongs, clamps, and a hammer.

"Fashioning a weapon that can dispatch a chimera," he replied as if such a thing were an everyday occurrence. But then, in this new world, maybe it was.

"And what weapon might that be?" I asked.

He answered by moving to a cupboard and opening the doors wide. Inside, a variety of weapons hung on display. With a sort of reverence, Vlad removed a gold inlaid crossbow and held it up.

"This," he answered. "With silver bolts."

He set about his task quickly, moving at a vampiric speed that would have been nothing but a blur to me before. But now, I could follow his every move. I watched with interest, absently running my tongue over my newly formed fangs. It was such an odd sensation, a little like a set of fake Halloween teeth.

"Can I help?" I asked after a bit, tired of staying on the sidelines like a wallflower.

Vlad captured my hand and gave it a kiss before handing me an iron bucket, filled to the brim with coal. "Here. Hold this while I light the fire."

The contents must have weighed a good eighty pounds, but now, to me, felt as light as a feather. I flexed my arm, impressed with my newfound strength.

Vlad smiled and then taking the coal from me, tossed it into the fireplace. After lighting the fire, he moved to a black, metal box near the wall, and using a pair of tongs, removed a silver bar.

"Silver is deadly, my love," he said, carefully carrying the accursed metal to the anvil. "To chimera, as well as ourselves."

"That's a bummer," I deadpanned. "You didn't mention I'd have to give up my silver jewelry. That might have been a deal breaker."

He glanced up, and I grinned and winked.

He huffed in annoyance. "I'll buy you all the gold and gemstone jewelry your heart could ever desire."

I joined him, but the closer I got to the silver bar,

sweat formed on my brow as a sudden nausea began to churn in my stomach.

"Think I'll just watch, for now," I said, returning to my place on the wall.

It wasn't so bad to watch. He took off his shirt to man the bellows, and I enjoyed observing the way his muscles worked. Under any other circumstances, I'd have pinned him down and had my way, but the constant undercurrent of worry over the creature my father had become doused any such thoughts before they burned too hot.

He worked quickly, using the tongs to heat the silver until it was red hot, and then poured it into the crossbow bolt molds.

"How long do you think we have?" I asked as he worked. "You know, before…" I didn't like calling a demon 'my father' or 'dad.' I didn't want to claim any kinship. So, I finished with, "Before the Creature comes here?"

Vlad looked up and his expression told me he understood. "He'll likely feed first." His gaze softened. "As you should."

Now that he mentioned it, I *was* thirsty. Or hungry? It was a sensation I'd never felt before. A burning in the back of my throat, dry and brutal. I'd been ignoring it, so absorbed by the Count and my new powers, but now it was all I could think about. Still, I wasn't leaving without him. No matter how much my throat begged for quenching.

"I'll wait for you," I said, eying the nearly completed row of silver bolts. "Is there a way to detect the Creature, when it arrives? What should I look for?"

"Leonard has the Shadows patrolling the grounds," he replied, adding the last bolt to the pile with a chink that brought back a resurgence of nausea. "They'll let us know."

That made me feel better, even though I didn't really understand. "These Shadows. Just what are they?"

"Sentient beings from another world. Protective. Dangerous. Yet, wanting love," the Count replied. He paused and settling his gaze on me, he added in a voice that felt like a caress, "Just like the rest of us."

I smiled. God, if only we didn't have to worry about some demonic creature coming after us. Would this be my life now? Or was this a one-off? Maybe we could get more of the Shadows to hang around. "Then, basically, they're your average Doberman?" I asked.

"Yes, somewhat like that," he chuckled.

Thinking of the shadows curled at Jeremy's feet, I asked, "But how is Jeremy involved with this?"

"Jeremy is a natural. It's a rare occurrence for Shadowmasters to be chosen from the human world." Vlad shook his head in wonder. "He needs training. At once."

His words made me realize that Jeremy needed to get back in school, but which one? And how could I ever answer calls from the front office if I slept like the dead during the day? I frowned. I'd have to deal. Somehow. "Don't think they teach Shadowmastery at your average junior high," I said.

The corner of Vlad's lip curled in a smile. "Not on Earth."

"You mentioned worlds before," I said, popping that item off the stack of questions to be asked. Now was as good as ever.

"And there are," he answered as he calmly collected the crossbow and the newly minted silver bolts. "Jeremy belongs in the Otherworld, and you, as well. There, you need not fear the sun."

On the way back to the house, as my thirst became more distracting, I peppered Vlad with questions about this Otherworld. "Where is this place?" I asked.

He held my hand as we walked, and I marveled at

the smoothness of his skin and the firmness of his grip. Every detail, every sensation felt amplified.

"No one really knows," he said. "It's a realm unto itself."

"And we'll be able to live there safely?"

He glanced down at me, a hint of sorrow in his eyes. "There is no true safety anywhere for creatures like us. But it does not hold the same perils as the human world."

"Why aren't you there?" I asked. "Not that I'm complaining."

"It is where Mary was murdered," he said.

"Shit. I'm so sorry." We walked in silence for a few moments before I spoke again. "We don't have to go back if it's too painful for you. We can make it work in this world somehow."

He paused and pulled me against his chest, holding me close as he spoke. "I would face anything to keep you and Jeremy safe. Memories cannot cause me harm. Not any longer. Not with you by my side."

We kissed deeply, but it was cut short by a shout coming from within the house.

I dashed in, my mind swirling frantically with worst case scenario thoughts. I slid to a stop at the kitchen door, Vlad by my side.

Jeremy stood at the island, laughing as a shadow

'fetched' a raw chicken leg to scurry back and drop it at his feet. The news played in the background on Jeremy's laptop, but no one was paying attention to the program.

"Very good," Leonard encouraged, a smile lighting up his face. "Now, give the command for him to eat it."

Jeremy closed his eyes but did not speak. Still, the shadow seemed to understand. With an audible poof, it surrounded the chicken, devouring it through smoke and mist until there was no trace left of meat or bone.

Leonard looked up at us, his glance landing on Vlad's. "He's quite powerful," he said. "Half of my clutch has bonded with him. I've never seen such a thing."

"Is this safe?" I asked, worry warring with my relief at seeing Jeremy so happy.

Vlad slipped an arm around my waist. "The shadows will protect him. He is safer with them than without, especially in this new world."

I could hear the words he didn't speak. That I had chosen to become a vampire, but if Jeremy were merely human, my new life wouldn't be safe for him. Now, with the shadows, he would be.

Jeremy looked up finally, his face beaming. "Did you see, Kassy? He's a good boy."

The shadow, as if in understanding, stood taller and seemed to puff out its chest in pride, even though it didn't actually have any discernable bodily features.

"Make sure you listen to Leonard and do what he says." I tried to make my voice mom-like but I was too happy for him to sound very firm.

Still, he nodded, his face serious. "I will. Promise."

Then he looked more closely at me, and his eyes seemed to fill with shadows for a moment before his jaw dropped. "You're a vampire!"

Vlad and I glanced at each other and Leonard raised an eyebrow. I had planned to tell Jeremy as soon as I could, but I wasn't expecting him to notice on his own.

"How could you tell?" I asked, squatting down to eye level with him.

He shrugged. "They help me see better."

Okay then.

"How do you feel about it?" I asked.

"It's cool. And you look happier. I like it. But... " he frowned. "Does that mean you don't want me anymore?"

My heart broke at his words, and I pulled him

into my arms. "I will always want you, buddy. You're mine. Mine and the Count's." I looked over to Vlad, who nodded and crouched on the kitchen floor, wrapping his arms around us both, as shadows danced around our legs like puppies.

Jeremy had tears in his eyes when we pulled away, and he looked up to Vlad. "You really want me too?"

Vlad nodded, and I swear even his dark eyes glistened. "Very much. If that is amendable to you?"

Jeremy's face split into a grin. "Very amendable."

I took a deep breath, relief flooding me that our little family was finally solid, but when the whiff of Jeremy's blood hit, I nearly choked. My fangs protruded and I panicked, pulling back.

"Vlad," I said, my eyes wild, my nails digging into the kitchen countertop, creating deep wedges in the marble.

He noticed my distress, as did Leonard. As Leonard placed himself protectively between me and Jeremy, Vlad used his speed to dash to the fridge and pull out a bottle of wine. When he uncorked it and poured it into a glass, I nearly expired right then and there. It smelled incredible. Now, I knew what the strange wine he'd always drank was. Blood.

The shadows around Jeremy had become agitated, forming a protective circle. "Don't worry," he cooed to them soothingly. "She won't hurt me, guys. It's okay."

I loved that he had such confidence in me, but right now, I didn't have it in myself. I needed blood. Badly.

The instant Vlad handed me a glass, I yanked it from his hand and chugged it down, letting the smooth, viscous liquid slide over my tongue and down my throat. The relief was instant. With the extra boost of energy, my senses heightened even more as my body relaxed, vanquishing the dryness in the back of my throat. Once I drained the glass, Vlad refilled it, and I continued drinking until the bottle was empty.

Then, I slumped against his chest, tears burning my eyes as my fingers shook. What if... what if... He brushed my hair back from my face as I struggled with emotions threatening to overwhelm me. "What if... " My throat caught.

Vlad's arms tightened, offering me silent support. "I wouldn't have let it happen. And it will get easier. Give it time."

It would get easier. That made sense. Vlad didn't walk around acting like a drug addict desperate for his next fix. But he'd been a vampire forever. "How long?"

"Quickly. It doesn't take long to adapt as long as you stay fed in the first few weeks. And I will make sure you stay fed." He paused. "And... if we feed on each other, you'll find you need less and less human blood."

His words inspired a wave of naughty imaginings that involved us naked, biting each other while exploring each other's bodies.

Just as I was about to find an excuse to drag him to the bedroom to satiate all my hungers, the red blinking 'Breaking News' banner on the laptop caught my attention.

"Jeremy, turn up the volume on your computer," I said, before realizing I didn't actually need him to. I could hear so much now, and yet, it didn't feel overwhelming. It was easy to 'turn up' or 'down' anything I wanted.

As 'Breaking News' continued to flash across the screen, the local newscaster began reporting on two women who had been found murdered in their own homes. In the same neighborhood my dad lived.

"The police haven't released the details of the crime, but early reports indicate it was a brutal attack. The women's throats were violently ripped out and their hearts appear to be missing."

Shit.

We all knew what it meant.

Vlad and I exchanged knowing glances as several shadows curled into little balls at Jeremy's feet. I really hoped his new little friends could protect him against this threat. A danger even Vlad seemed worried about.

"Did Dad do that?" Jeremy asked, his voice small.

"That's not Dad anymore," I told him. "It's something evil. A monster that wants to hurt us. It's not him."

It was a weak argument, and we both knew it. Our father had always been a monster who wanted to hurt us. Now, this version had more power to do so. But the damage he'd already done to our hearts was worse than anything this creature could do to our bodies.

Vlad's body stiffened beside me, and he shifted his head slightly.

I was about to ask him what he'd heard when I heard it myself.

A cry, like a howl, followed by an unholy hiss coming from somewhere outside.

The creature had arrived.

20

"*I* shall return," Vlad said as he grabbed the crossbow from the counter and turned to leave.

"I'm going with you," I announced. I felt strong. Powerful. Unstoppable. And I wouldn't let him fight my enemies alone.

He drew an admiring breath. "Come." He held out his hand. "But if you find him, you will not take him by yourself."

"I promise."

Leonard followed us to the front door, his shadows dancing at his feet.

Jeremy knew better than to ask if he could join. He returned to his stool at the island. "I'll just play fetch and train them some more," he offered.

"Stay inside," I ordered.

As he nodded, Leonard raised a hand. At once, a shadow dashed out the door and came back so fast, even with my vampire vision I barely noticed it.

"They detected something on the north side of the house," Leonard announced.

"Shall we run?" Vlad asked, a grin on his handsome, chiseled face.

"Yes!" Despite the gravity of the situation, I looked forward to stretching my vampire wings, as it were.

And so we ran. The wind whipped through my hair and I relished my newfound incredible speed and dexterity. I felt like a superhero and I knew I would never regret my choice to turn. Not only was Vlad worth it all, but this, how I felt, this incredible euphoria, it was worth anything I might have left behind. I'd never felt more alive than now, and the irony was not lost on me. My life truly began the moment my heart stopped.

We circled the mansion a few times, ensuring nothing was out of place, just as a precaution, even though I knew Leonard and the shadows would watch after Jeremy.

Then, we ran.

After doing a complete inspection of the property, we paused by the rose garden.

"Nothing," Vlad said.

"False alarm?" I asked, not even a little out of breath.

"There are many creatures of the night," he said. "Not all are friendly."

"That's reassuring," I said dryly. "When this is all over, I'm gonna need some kind of crash course on this new life. Maybe 'How to be a Vampire for Dummies' or something?"

He chuckled but stopped abruptly the moment we turned the corner of the house to see the front door standing open, light from the hallway spilling out.

Then, I saw him.

Leonard, lying in the driveway, lifeless.

"Jeremy?" I screamed, dashing into the house. I hated to leave Leonard, but I had to save my brother.

Halfway to the kitchen, I drew up short.

Through the window to the backyard I saw Jeremy walking slowly towards the woods. He seemed hypnotized. Even his shadows behaved strangely, following him like lifeless snakes. I screamed his name, but he couldn't hear me through the double-paned glass.

I dashed to the back door and threw it open, my eyes easily adjusting to the darkness.

Jeremy had stopped before a figure standing at the edge of the trees in the moonlight.

My heart leapt into my throat. It had been so long since I'd seen her face, that smile.

"Mom?"

"No," Vlad hissed, wrapping me in his arms from behind, holding me back. Then, raising his voice, he called out, "Jeremy, stop. That is not your mother."

I felt sick. So, the creature could take on other forms? That would have been useful information to have. "Jeremy!" I screamed, "Come back!"

I jerked out of Vlad's arms and ran outside.

Vlad followed, his crossbow raised. "I can't get a clear shot, not from here. Not without endangering Jeremy."

I flew as fast as my new powers would let me, toward Jeremy and the creature. It looked so much like her. Her long dark hair almost glowed under the full moon. Every feature, down to her favorite blue dress and her heart shaped face were exactly as I remembered.

Everything but the eyes.

There was no soul in her eyes. Only evil.

"Leave him alone!"

The creature looked up and smiled, the cruel smile of a thing without conscience.

I was so close, only a few yards away. "That's not mom, Jeremy," I hissed.

He didn't listen. It was like he was sleep walking. As I watched, the figure reached for him, arms opening wide. And even though the shadows trembled at Jeremy's feet, he stepped forward into her embrace.

Then, everything seemed to move in slow motion.

The woman's arms turned into claws. Mutated body parts began to pop out from her neck, spine, and legs, transforming her into a hideous beast of mismatched animal parts that looked like it had been put together in Frankenstein's lab.

Suddenly, the claws slashed through the air.

Blood splatter hit the creature's face as Jeremy's small body crashed to the ground.

My heart froze. I couldn't think. I could only stare in shock at his crumpled form lying in the damp grass.

Time seemed to stand still.

And as if I had been the one attacked, my life with my little brother flashed before my eyes. I relived all of our memories together in a fraction of a heartbeat, even as Vlad took his shot.

As the silver bolt sliced the air straight and true, to pierce the very center of the beast's heart, all I could think about were the nights I'd spent reading Jeremy to sleep while he curled in my arms.

As the creature screamed, falling back with a howl of anguish, the death cry of a wounded animal, my mine recalled cherished memories of teaching my brother how to ride a bike, and how much it hurt *me* every time he fell and bruised his knees. But he would just laugh and tell me he was tougher than he looked.

As the creature staggered and dropped to its knees, I was lost in the memory of the Christmas I saved all my waitressing money to get Jeremy the microscope he had been hoping for. The look in his eyes made all the hours of sacrifice worth it.

As the monster breathed its last breath, I stayed rooted in shock. I'd promised Jeremy I'd keep him safe. That I'd protect him. My heart tore at the impotence of my lie.

Then, I was rushing to his side, hysterical tears blinding my vision. I fell to my knees and pulled him into my arms. Blood gushed from his throat, and his wide brown eyes began to gloss over as he tried to speak.

"No! No!" I sobbed, trying in vain to stop the blood.

Jeremy gurgled, spitting crimson.

I had no choice. I had to make him a vampire. To save his life. In that moment, I didn't even care if he wanted that or not. I wouldn't let him die. I couldn't lose him. My tears mingled with his blood as I prepared myself.

But just as I leaned into him to begin, I noticed the wound on his throat had stopped bleeding.

"No," I gasped. I was too late.

Yet even as I thought my deepest fear, I felt his heart beat. It was faint, ever so faint, but still there.

And he was breathing.

It was then, with my new vision, that I saw every detail of the shadows curling around him, covering his throat. Tendrils of smoke writhed over the wound, stitching it closed. Healing him.

I held my breath as his eyelashes fluttered and he blinked. "It wasn't Mom," he whispered, his cheeks wet with tears.

"No, baby," I choked, hugging him close. "It wasn't. But I'm here forever and you're going to be okay."

He reached up and returned my hug, the strength coming back to him faster than I could have ever imagined. I just held him, hugging him close.

Gradually, I became aware of the creature, lifeless

on the ground with Vlad standing over it, crossbow still in hand.

"Is it over?" I asked.

"Yes." He nodded and then looked over his shoulder as Leonard limped into view, injured but upright.

Jeremy pulled himself from my arms, and though I was reluctant to let go, I eased my grip so he could turn to look at Leonard. "They fixed me," he blurted.

Leonard responded with a solemn nod. "They are yours and you are theirs."

Doubtless, the shadows explained why Leonard was also still alive right now. His shadows had healed him, too, just like Jeremy.

I glanced at Vlad, bending over the body of the creature. When he straightened again, I saw that he'd cut off its head and removed its heart. Black blood stained his clothing and skin, and as he moved, currents of air brought the foul stench of putrid demon blood to my nostrils.

"Breathing is optional," Vlad told me, catching the look on my face. "If you wish to avoid the stench."

Testing his claim, I held my breath. It felt awkward and unnatural, but he was right. I didn't actually need air. Interesting.

257

Curious, I joined him to study what remained of the body. There was little left and nothing of it resembled the father I knew. For as much relief as I'd felt at his death, I wished for both our sakes he could have been a better person. A better parent.

"Do you need time to say goodbye?" Vlad murmured at my side.

I turned to Jeremy, who shook his head.

We were both more than ready to let go. "No," I said simply.

Then, Leonard gave the command, and the shadows arrived to swarm over the creature's remains, devouring him.

Jeremy and I watched our father's body pass before us for the last time. He'd caused us both a wealth of pain, but as evil as he'd been our entire lives, he'd given us the gift of each other. And for that, I would always be grateful.

With all traces of the monster gone, the four of us walked slowly back to the house, exhausted. Even with my super strength, I was emotionally and mentally spent.

I took care of Jeremy first and walked with him to his room. I was going to insist on a shower, but he collapsed into his bed and was asleep before his head hit the pillow. I settled for tucking him in as his shadows curled around his head and shoulders.

Content that he was in good care, I went to grab a change of clothes, but all my things were gone. Confused, I went to Vlad's room next only to find him hanging my clothes in the closet next to his.

"I hope you do not mind," he said. "I can put them back if you'd like. But you're no longer my house-keeper. You are my mate, and I want you with me." He paused, and then added softly, "If that's acceptable."

It was touching to see the Count, so strong and powerful, suddenly unsure and a little shy.

I smiled. "Being with you is all I want."

Slowly, he approached me and helped me undress. I did the same for him, and we tossed the soiled clothes into the trash bin to be burned. Then Vlad started the shower and drew me under the water with him. We just stood there, arms entwined, letting the hot water cleanse the stain of death.

It was hard to believe it was over. Finally, actually over.

The Count reached for the soap and ran his hands over my body, gently washing me, caressing me. With closed eyes, I leaned into him, savoring the moment, the feeling of being loved, cared for.

Once we were both as clean as we could get, we dried, and I slipped into one of his softest t-shirts as Vlad donned a pair of sweatpants and we both crawled into bed.

I felt the sun break over the horizon, sensing it deep in my soul. My eyes grew heavy and began to close of their own accord.

"Rest now, my love," Vlad whispered into my hair, wrapping his arms around me. "Tomorrow we will start our new life."

I smiled, knowing I was safe in his embrace and with a sigh, let sleep steal me away.

21

I woke to the scent of roses. Their perfume reminded me of a summer day, something that would forever be a memory to me now.

Soft lips brushed my collarbone.

I smiled and burrowed deeper against the solid wall of muscle at my back. Who needed summers when I could live in the warmth of Vlad's love for an eternity? What more could I ask for in life?

His lips returned, making their way up my neck. I held still under the gentle assault, reveling in what it felt like to be loved, completely, as I was.

"Good evening," Vlad whispered, nuzzling the soft flesh under my ear.

I lifted my lashes to see him staring down at me

with that sexy grin creasing his cheek. "Same to you," I said.

There was too much cloth between us. Me, in my t-shirt. Him, in sweatpants. I wanted the primal closeness of flesh on flesh. Still, I smiled and shifted lazily on my back.

"Kiss me," I demanded, but his lips covered mine before I'd even finished uttering the last word.

For a time, we simply enjoyed the dancing of our tongues, but then, our hands began to roam. He kneaded my breasts, pinching my nipples beneath my t-shirt as I slipped my hand beneath the waistband of his pants.

He was hard, ready. And I was impatient.

I bit his neck.

He threw his head back and gasped.

I smiled, pleased with his reaction.

"On your back," I demanded, placing my palms on his chest and shoving him back.

He complied with a smile crooking his lips. God, I loved his mouth. It looked carved as if from stone.

As I lifted my leg over his lean hips, he grabbed my waist and pulled me toward his mouth.

"God," I gasped, as his tongue caressed me. I grabbed the headboard; grateful I'd gone to bed the night before sans panties. What a way to start the day —err, evening.

He gripped my ass tighter, pulling me closer as his tongue worked magic, radiating pleasure to the end of my every nerve.

"Don't stop," I groaned, feeling my orgasm building.

He didn't. And when he grazed the softness of my inner flesh with his fangs, I climaxed. I held onto the headboard, a gasping, writhing tangle of sensations, him licking me all the while.

When I finally held still, he pulled me down across his chest and sat up, the movement sending me sprawling backwards onto the bed.

"With the appetizer finished, is it not now time for the main course?" he murmured, lifting a brow over lust-hazed eyes.

"Absolutely." I couldn't agree more. I rose to my knees and ran my hand over his arousal, smiling in anticipation.

He closed his eyes, his lips parting in pleasure as I teased him, sliding my hands over his every inch. I studied his face, reveling in having him under my control, hanging on my every move. This was Count Dracula. My lover. The love of my life.

I wanted nothing between us, no barriers of any

kind, mental or physical. So, I pulled off his sweat-pants and then, my t-shirt as well, and slowly lowered myself onto him.

God, I belonged with him. I'd never felt so complete. As we began to move, I ran my hands over his chest, outlining the bands of muscle, tracing the lines of his veins running across his flesh.

My eyes caught on his veins. God, I needed to taste him again. My fangs descended as I dropped myself over his hard body and sank my teeth into his neck.

He tasted finer than any wine I'd ever had, satis-fying my cravings like nothing else could. A drug I could live on for life. I drove my fangs deeper, feeding and drawing his blood as he inhaled and thrust into me harder, faster, again and again.

Then, with a growl, he flipped me onto my back and drove himself into me with such force that I wrapped my legs around him, digging my nails into his back to hold on. And when his fangs pierced my flesh, I never felt more alive.

He roared as he finished, the sound tipping me into my own waves of pleasure.

Finally, when the last traces of our love faded away, he propped himself on an elbow, and reached over me to pluck a red rose from the vase on the bedside table.

Gently, he trailed the soft velvet petals over my lips, my throat, my breasts. Teasing my nipples into hardened peaks.

"Enough torture," I growled, already ready for another go.

Lust entered his dark, expressive eyes as he whispered, "I want you, Kassandra. Forever."

EPILOGUE

*I*f you're still reading this, then you already know the fate that befell me the day I walked into the Count's mansion for a job as his housekeeper with the intent of robbing him blind.

I thought I would end up dead. That Don or my father would kill me, one way or another. I never imagined I would live a long life—that's just not a future I believed I had access to.

It turns out, my life will be a hell of a lot longer than anyone could have imagined. Including myself.

I did die.

And then I was reborn.

I am stronger. Faster. More powerful than any human.

And I am safe. Or as safe as I've ever been.

And loved.

It's not a rainbows and unicorns kind of love.

It's a dark loved filled with the stars of twilight and the secrets of lost magic. It's a love made of blood and violence and pain. A love that walks in the shadows. It's not a love for everyone, but it's a love for me. For him. For us. The only kind of love either of us could embrace and hold onto. Any other love would have slipped through our fingers, turning to dust. This love, it is hard and heavy and forever.

The Count—Vlad—sweeps into the room, his long black cloak swishing behind him dramatically. He surveys the space. All the furniture is draped in protective cloth. Personal items have been removed. Valuables packed up. The rest will be left until this town ages into its own forgetfulness.

Memory is fleeting.

But vampires are forever.

We will return. When it's safe. When the blood spilled and lives lost had faded to smudged ink in a forgotten newspaper.

He drapes an arm around my shoulder and pulls me closer to him. "Are you ready?"

I nod. There's a lump in my throat and my hands tremble slightly, but I tilt my face to his, seeking his lips.

His kisses always undo me in the best possible way, and I need to be undone right now, so I can be remade in our new life together.

Jeremy and I will begin new lives with Vlad and Leonard. We will all leave this world and set up home in the Otherworld.

As if on cue, my little brother skids into the living room, his arms full of unpacked clothing. "I forgot a few things," he says sheepishly.

The shadows at his feet pause when he does, waiting patiently for the most part, like newly trained puppies who still struggle to stay still but are doing their level best.

Vlad smiles and Leonard rushes into the room with an extra bag, which he quickly uses to pack Jeremy's clothes.

Leonard stands, his own shadows waiting patiently behind him. They are as calm and focused as the Shadowmaster himself, and I imagine what Jeremy and his shadows will become as he grows into his own powers. It's a heady thought.

"Can we go now? I don't want to be late for my first day of school!" He tugs at the Count's hand, and the ancient vampire indulges him, allowing himself to be dragged forward.

"Yes, it is time to say goodbye."

In another world, a new life awaits us. A magical school that trains kids like Jeremy. Kids born into paranormal power. He will be safe there and given the kind of education he needs. And we will be a family.

We step out of the mansion and Leonard locks the door behind us, then the four of us walk towards the car, the shadows nipping at our heels, memories of what has been haunting the imaginings of what's to come. And I smile, happy to let my old life die so I can truly live in my new one.

Forever.

Wanted.

ABOUT KARPOV KINRADE

Karpov Kinrade is the pen name for the husband and wife writing duo of USA TODAY bestselling, award-winning authors Lux Karpov-Kinrade and Dmytry Karpov-Kinrade.

Together, they live in Ukiah, California and write novels and screenplays, make music and direct movies.

Look for more from Karpov Kinrade in *The Night Firm*, *Vampire Girl*, *Of Dreams and Dragons*, *Nightfall Academy* and *Paranormal Spy Academy*. If you're looking for their suspense and romance titles, you'll now find those under Alex Lux.

They live with their three teens who share a genius for all things creative, and seven cats who think they rule the world (spoiler, they do.)

Want their books and music before anyone else (plus you'll gain access to weekly interactive flash fiction?) Join them on Patreon at Patreon.com/karpovkinrade

Find them online at KarpovKinrade.com

On Facebook /KarpovKinrade

On Twitter @KarpovKinrade

And subscribe to their newsletter at ReadKK.com for special deals and up-to-date notice of new launches.

~ ~ ~ ~ ~

If you enjoyed this book, consider supporting the author by leaving a review wherever you purchased this book. Thank you.

facebook.com/karpovkinrade

twitter.com/karpovkinrade

ABOUT LIV CHATHAM

For Liv Chatham, one life is not enough, but she solved that problem by living vicariously through her characters in fantastic worlds. When she's not reading, she's biking to the nearest coffee shop to cuddle with a latte and write, and then she's biking back home again to cuddle with her French Bulldog and write some more. Since she doesn't like to hold still, she doesn't stay long in one place, and because she's naturally nosy, she's lived and travelled in over forty countries around the world. By nature, she's a fantasy and paranormal addict, but since she's never met a word she didn't like, she'll dabble in other genres from time to time.

Sign up for Liv's newsletter at LivChatham.com and become her friend at …

FB: /author.liv.chatham

Dungeon Queen

Warrior Queen

The Night Firm

I Am the Wild

I Am the Storm

I Am the Night

Wanted

Wanted 2

Wanted 3

In the Vampire Girl Universe

Vampire Girl

Vampire Girl 2: Midnight Star

Vampire Girl 3: Silver Flame

Vampire Girl 4: Moonlight Prince

Vampire Girl 5: First Hunter

Vampire Girl 6: Unseen Lord

Vampire Girl 7: Fallen Star

Vampire Girl: Copper Snare

Vampire Girl: Crimson Cocktail

Vampire Girl: Christmas Cognac

Of Dreams and Dragons

Get the soundtrack for I AM THE WILD, OF DREAMS AND DRAGONS and MOONSTONE ACADEMY wherever music can be found.

Nightfall Academy

Court of Nightfall

Weeper of Blood

House of Ravens

Night of Nyx

Song of Kai

Daughter of Strife

Paranormal Spy Academy (complete academy sci fi thriller romance)

Forbidden Mind

Forbidden Fire

Forbidden Life

Our ALEX LUX BOOKS!

The Seduced Saga (paranormal romance with suspense)

Seduced by Innocence

Seduced by Pain

Seduced by Power

Seduced by Lies

Seduced by Darkness

The Call Me Cat Trilogy (romantic suspense)

Call Me Cat

Leave Me Love

Tell Me True

(Standalone romcon with crossover characters)

Hitched

Whipped

Kiss Me in Paris (A standalone romance)

Our Children's Fantasy collection under Kimberly Kinrade

The Three Lost Kids series

Lexie World

Bella World

Maddie World

The Three Lost Kids and Cupid's Capture

The Three Lost Kids and the Death of the Sugar Fairy

The Three Lost Kids and the Christmas Curse

Made in the USA
Las Vegas, NV
30 March 2021